THE LIAR
I MARRIED

BOOKS BY D.K. HOOD

THE LIAR
I MARRIED

D.K. HOOD

bookouture

Published by Bookouture in 2025

An imprint of Storyfire Ltd.
Carmelite House
50 Victoria Embankment
London EC4Y 0DZ

www.bookouture.com

The authorised representative in the EEA is Hachette Ireland
8 Castlecourt Centre
Dublin 15 D15 XTP3
Ireland
(email: info@hbgi.ie)

ISBN: 978-1-83618-731-8
eBook ISBN: 978-1-83618-730-1

Everyone needs a hero, someone who protects, encourages, and stands beside them no matter what the future holds. Mine is my wonderful husband, Gary. This one is for you.

PROLOGUE

Images of *her* kissing my husband slam into my brain. How could he do this to me? I need to get away. I can't think straight. My mind is screaming at me to, "Drive, drive, drive." The way ahead blurs from my tears and my brand-new SUV swerves across the blacktop, tires screaming. Headlights cut through the darkness, illuminating flashes of brown and green trees alongside the highway. The steering wheel is slippery under my palms. I can't move it and panic grips me as I fight to gain control. The car accelerates and someone is yelling abuse at me so close to my ear it hurts. A burst of pain spears my temple, jolting my head to one side. Pinwheels of light dance in front of my eyes but I hold tight to the wheel. Blinking frantically, I fight the vehicle's uncontrollable slide across the road. My hands ache as I wrench the steering wheel away from trees coming closer by the second. I must regain control. Please God help me —my girls are asleep in the back! The SUV responds for a second before it speeds up again. I stab my foot down hard on the pedal. Nothing. Why can't I make the brakes work?

Terror grips me. I don't know what to do: my new car is like a runaway train. My seatbelt bites into my shoulder as violent swerves toss me from one side to the other. The yelling is getting louder. Who is in the car with me? I can't take my eyes from the road to see. The yellow line is a slithering snake and my arm muscles tear from their sockets but I won't give in. I'm fighting for my life. Somehow, I make it around the next bend but my car fishtails. I'm sliding sideways and heading straight for a tree. The engine roars like some evil being has taken over. I can't stop it.

Someone is screaming—is it me? The tree is there right in front of me. A deafening bang and a shattering jolt throws my head back, wrenching my neck. I'm flying forward, my teeth slam together and I taste blood in my mouth. Windows explode and glass shatters like diamonds. Metal grinds and a cloud of suffocating white hits my face. The back of the car bounces as it settles on the blacktop. A horn shrieks and then silence. Darkness is closing in around me. *Where are my kids?*

ONE

I remember the perfect times. When I look at my handsome husband, John, and wonder why he chose me. You see, he turns heads everywhere he goes and—a gorgeous stockbroker—he's not only the epitome of success but his charm is legendary too. Our marriage, now eight years strong, is like a fairy tale. We have beautiful six-year-old twins, Emily and Olivia, who bring joy and laughter into our lives every day. We purchased a house in Grande Haven, an upmarket gated community, which is a sanctuary, a place where love and happiness thrives. My life with John is perfect—a society couple, with a joining of wealth and position everyone envies—but I know for certain we married for love. Our lives together are like a magazine center spread of a loving devoted couple. Well, this was the case until recently. Now everything is falling like dominoes.

The man who couldn't wait to get home to me now comes home late—if he comes home at all. The excuses are always the same—late meetings, urgent client calls, and more frequently the unexpected business trips. At first, I believed him. Why shouldn't I? His dedication to his work means we live here, in absolute luxury. I can stay at home with my kids, play tennis, or go out for lunch, but lately, doubt has started to creep in, like the grim reaper lurking in the corners of my mind.

Pushing the bad thoughts away, I try to focus on the good times. I'll never forget the way John used to look at me with love burning in his eyes. He'd tell me over and over again how I was his world. I loved the way he played with the girls, making them giggle with his silly antics. Each day, he's becoming more remote. He comes home, falls into bed, and is asleep in seconds but then gone before I wake. He hasn't spoken to the girls in weeks and the distance between us is growing by the second.

I can't help but wonder if he's having an affair. The thought gnaws at me, keeping me awake at night, even when he's beside me, his back turned away, I lie in bed, staring at the ceiling. I replay every interaction, every conversation, searching for clues, but I'm falling into an abyss of confusion and questioning everything.

I walk into the family room and the silence is deafening. The girls are asleep, and the house is an empty vessel without John's presence. I used to love this room and spent endless hours making it perfect. From the soft sofas with matching throws and scattered cushions, right down to the little nook, with a table and bookcase where the girls can play. I sit and stare out over the landscaped gardens and see the moon reflected in the pool—a big blue-white orb in a cloudless sky. Everything is so tranquil but my mind is in turmoil. The quiet is eating me up and the soft hum of the refrigerator and the distant ticking of the grandfather clock are the only sounds that break the silence. I lift my phone from the coffee table; my fingers tremble as I scroll through John's messages. They are short, to the point, and the emojis he always loves to add are missing as if someone is reading them over his shoulder, and that only makes me more suspicious. He's too careful, too meticulous.

I can't speak to my friends; it would be all over town in twenty-four hours. The last time we had a fight, his mother turned up to act as referee. That woman will never understand her little boy is a grown man now and doesn't need her to fight his battles. I need to talk to someone but who can I confide in? My brother, Michael, has always been my rock, the one person I trust completely. I make the call. "Can you come over? I need to talk to you. I need advice."

"Yeah, sure. I'll be there in twenty." Michael disconnects.

Indecision now plagues me. Am I making too much out of a feeling? I head to the kitchen and brew a pot of coffee. The box of fresh pastries I'd purchased for our once-regular movie night sits on the table untouched and I flip open the lid. The aroma of freshly brewed coffee mingles with the scent of the pastries, but I shut the box, unable to eat.

The doorbell chimes and my brother greets me with a hug. We sit at the kitchen table and I tell him my concerns and show him the messages. Michael listens patiently, and his brow furrows with worry. I push the pastries toward him. "Do you figure I'm making too much of this?"

"Jessie, you need to talk to him." Michael's voice is like a soothing balm to my frayed nerves. "You can't let this stress you out like this. It'll eat you alive."

The thought of confronting John terrifies me. I shake my head. "I can't. What if I'm wrong? What if I'm right? Either way, our lives will never be the same." I stare at him. "We have a prenup. If we divorce, I'll only have what I brought into the marriage and that's gone now."

"Are you saying, all this is his, and he never gave you anything?" Michael's eyes widen. "I figured he loved you."

I wipe a hand down my face. "Obviously not enough to be faithful. I can't prove he's cheating on me. It might be all in my mind, but he did come home stinking of perfume and he said it was from a client he shared a cab with. Now I'm not so sure." I look at him and tears sting my eyes. "Am I imagining all this because I'm lonely and need to blame someone? You've always said I have an overactive imagination. I'm starting to question my sanity right now."

"All I can say, being in the same business, is that the higher we want to climb, the harder we need to work." Michael reaches for a pastry. "I know John has clients lining up for representation. He makes them money and is moving up through the firm faster than anyone else. I have women clients as well and they hit on me all the time." He takes a bite of the pastry and hums in appreciation.

That piece of information hasn't helped my troubled mind. "He gets women hitting on him all the time and I've never felt like this before. We had date nights and he made time to be with me but that's stopped. He doesn't touch me anymore. Men need sex, right? So where is he getting his supply?"

"Whoa." Michael holds the pastry midway to his mouth. "That's not something I need to know, Jessie." He sighs. "Look, I'll do some detective work and see if I can find out anything but remember, he's way above my pay grade. I don't want to lose my job by snooping but I'll see what I can find out. Okay?"

My stomach drops. Finding out the truth, if he *is* having an affair, will break my heart. "Then what will I do if he wants a divorce? I've got nowhere to go, no money, no job."

"Mom and Dad will get you settled some other place if you don't want to return home. I can help too, so don't worry about that. You do what feels right." Michael pats my hand. "I hate to say it but we both know Grandma isn't long for this world and Mom will inherit a fortune. Mom has been spending every day sitting with her. You should go and see her, before it's too late." He sighs. "You know how much she dotes on you."

The thought of losing my grandma makes my heart ache. My safe havens, the people I love, are vanishing like mist in the morning sunshine. My world is crumbling around me. Lost in my thoughts, I realize this is the beginning of a journey that will unravel everything I believe I knew about my life, my marriage, and myself.

TWO

NOW

Beep, beep, beep.

I'm here in the darkness but where is here? I try to move my legs but they're heavy as if stuck in thick black tar. Am I dead? Is this what death feels like? In my personal darkness I drag in a breath and feel the air flowing out of my nose. Maybe not dead then. My eyelids are heavy, so heavy as if they'd been taped down, but I try to force them open. A blinding light comes through my eyelashes. Is this the light I must follow? My brain is muddled; how did I end up dead? What is that beeping sound? It's starting to drive me insane.

My tongue moves in a dry mouth and swats across cracked lips. Perhaps I've been frozen and I'm slowly thawing. I must concentrate harder to open my eyes. Suddenly, light comes in a blur of color, and moving patterns dance across my vision. Green and brown leopard spots mingle with sparkling orbs as they wave back and forth. Slowly my eyes adjust to the light and I see a window in front of me and, beyond, the branches of a tree in fall. I see a garden and rose bushes. I know this place. A memory of picking roses with my mom and bringing armfuls into the house drifts past like smoke. I want to see more but my lids are heavy and drop down, obscuring my view. It's been an effort to concentrate as if I'm drugged, or coming out of heavy sedation. After surgery for a broken ankle, I remember how difficult it was to wake up. Maybe this is what's happened? I don't remember.

When I open my eyes again, darkness presses against the window. A small light glows on a table and I recognize the thick brocade drapes held with a gold rope through copper rings set in the window frame. The memories are coming back now. I'm in my grandmother's house, in the sunroom overlooking the garden. What has happened to me? I try to think but a fog obscures the details. It's like trying to catch shadows. The maddening *beep, beep, beep* is still there. "Turn off the noise." A voice I don't recognize escapes my lips. It's little more than a raspy scratchy whisper.

"Oh, good, you're awake." The face of a young woman, blonde hair tied back at the nape of the neck, stares at me and then snaps on a pair of examination gloves. "Would you like a drink?"

I manage a nod and a straw slides between my lips. Cold water slips like nectar down my throat but it's taken away before my thirst is quenched. My gaze moves over the woman again trying to recall who she is, but I'm sure I don't know her. She's dressed in a blue shirt, with a gray cardigan over a matching skirt that covers her knees and comfortable slip-on shoes. The noise thankfully stops and I stare at her as she checks a machine beside the bed. I lift a heavy arm to touch my face and she grabs it, placing it back down beside me.

"You'll pull out your drip." She looks at me, her face critical. "I'm Dolly, your nurse. You've been out for a long time... what's the last thing you remember?"

It came back in a rush of terror, the dark winding road, the grinding of metal... my twin daughters were in the car. I try to sit up but she presses me back down on the bed. "My kids. Where are they? Are they okay? I was dreaming about a car wreck and I drove into a tree. That doesn't matter now. All that matters are my kids. Where are they?"

She just looks at me as if I've asked her to fly around the room or something. What has happened? My heart pounds. Her indifference is infuriating. "Where's John? Is he okay?"

"Your husband is fine." Dolly patted my hand and smiled. "I'll call him and he'll be right along."

So she gives out information about John but not my kids. What's going on here? I look at her and grip her arm as much as I can. "I need to know if my kids are okay. Tell me."

"Stay calm, Jessie. I'm just a nurse, I don't know any details about your personal life. The only contact I have is your husband, okay? I do know you've been in a coma and mustn't upset yourself. Everything will be okay." The nurse moves away and then returns with a needle and presses the tip into the tubing running to a plastic bag of something hanging from a stand.

I try to fight to stay awake but the drugs drag me into oblivion. *Where are my kids?*

A voice reaches through the haze. I'm swimming against giant waves, fighting against the drugs. My head weighs a ton, and trying to move is impossible, but I'm awake. It's an effort to clear the fog from my mind. The last thing I remember is the nurse sticking the needle into my drip.

"Jessie?" A familiar voice close by drags me back to full consciousness. "It's me, John. Do you remember me? I'm your husband."

Of course I know him, he's been haunting my dreams. I turn

my head slowly, to find John standing by the door, as polished as ever in his tailored suit. His face is a mask of concern, but his once-loving eyes are empty. A flood of memories hit me in a confused muddle. He looks fine but some part of my consciousness insists he was in the car with me when I crashed. Now I'm confused. If I ended up in a coma, how did he walk away without a scratch? What part of my memories is dreams and what is the truth?

I push words through a dry and scratchy throat. "John." I blink at him, trying to focus.

"Do you remember what happened?" John's intense expression frightens me.

I don't remember but I look at him. "Just before, I had a dream about a car wreck." I see the truth in his face. Alarm grips me and my hands shake. "It's true? I wrecked the car? Oh, God no! Where are the girls? Are Emily and Olivia okay? Did you bring them with you?" Tears wet my cheeks and I desperately need a hug. I stretch out my hand toward him but when he doesn't move, I drop it and wait for him to speak. Something unspeakable has happened.

"You don't remember anything at all about that night?" John searches my face. "Only a dream?"

I nod and sniffle. "In the dream I'm fighting to keep the SUV on the road and hit a tree then I wake up. Everything else is blank. Tell me what happened. Where are my girls?" I grip his arm, digging in my nails. "Tell me, dammit."

"You need to rest, Jessie." John hesitates, a flicker of something—guilt?—crossing his face. "Don't worry about anything right now."

I struggle to sit up, but my body refuses to cooperate. "Don't worry? They're our babies, John. I need to know if they're okay."

"I'm not allowed to tell you anything, Jessie, so please, don't upset yourself. The doctor insists it will all come back to you soon. The answers are inside your head, and we've all been instructed to allow that to happen for your own good. The doctors said it will take time to get your head straight. You need to trust me. Everything will be fine. Just focus on getting better." He sits on the edge of the bed but doesn't hold me; he just places a hand on my arm. It's meant to be comforting, but feels like a restraint.

Unable to believe my ears, I stare at him. His empty words do nothing to soothe my anxiety. "This is crazy... not knowing makes me upset. John, *please*, I need to know."

"I can't." He shakes his head. "I'm sorry."

He actually looks remorseful as if I'm hurting him. I lower my voice to make him see reason. "Why won't you tell me where they are? Why aren't they here?"

"Jessie, *please*. You've just woken from a coma. You need to take it easy. Getting upset will mean you need to be sedated and that will delay recovery. It's better to allow everything to come back naturally. I don't know what happened, Jessie, it's locked inside your head." John's grip tightens slightly and his face pales. "I'll help you fill in the blanks when you start to recover. Right now, I need you to get better, darling. I miss you."

As I search his face, looking for answers, all I see is a carefully constructed facade. "I remember things from before the accident, John. I remember you missing your birthday dinner I'd prepared especially."

"I can't change the past, Jessie." He sighs. "But I'm here now."

Memories tumble through my mind in a muddled stream of information. I don't know what's real and what's an illusion. For some reason I'm angry with him—why? Do I blame him for the accident? Where did that come from? An image of him with a beautiful woman slides across my consciousness making me gasp.

Words spill from my mouth. "You should have been here when I woke the first time. You're never around, John. Even before the accident, you were always working late or not coming home at all." I can't stop the words tumbling out. "Are you seeing someone else?"

"No!" He recoils slightly, his expression hardening. "Of course not. We have a wonderful marriage. Why would I spoil it?"

I cough, my throat closing. "Then why aren't you ever home?"

"You knew when we married my work would take up a good deal of my time. I wanted to succeed to give you the life-style you deserved." He wipes a hand down his face. "That takes sacrifices and family time is one of them."

I look at him, tears welling. "I needed you, John, and now I need answers and you refuse to give them to me. I thought you loved me?"

"You know I do. Look, this isn't the time to argue, Jessie." John holds a straw to my lips. "I give you everything you need. Most women would be grateful. You live like a queen because I work hard. What you're saying is unfair." He blows out a long sigh and lowers the glass. "I didn't have time to just drop by, in case you *might* wake up. I've been waiting for a miracle for almost a year; each time I come it's a false alarm. It's an hour's drive from my work. I have important clients to see. Can you imagine how long I'd last at the firm if I kept canceling appointments? My reputation would be ruined."

I manage to get to my elbows and glare at him. "Then when is the right time? I've been lying here, wondering if my children are alive, and you won't give me a straight answer." I meet his gaze. "That nurse won't tell me anything." I shake my head slowly. "All I know now is it wasn't a dream. I hit a tree. I'm awake now, you can't break me, John. I need to know what's happening." I grip his arm. "*Please.* I need to know about the girls." Tears stream down my cheeks and I hiccup between sobs. "*Please*, John."

"Not yet, Jessie. You need more time. We need to start back a ways and come forward slowly. That's what the doctor advised; speaking about the car wreck can cause damage." John sighs and untangles my arm. "Do you remember your grand-mother's death?" He looks away and runs a hand through his perfectly styled hair before returning his gaze. "You attended the reading of her will, here in the study."

The question catches me off guard. "What does that have to do with anything?"

"Just answer the question, Jessie." John's eyes bore into me. "Do you remember?"

I close my eyes, trying to piece together the fragments of my memory. My grandmother's funeral, the somber faces, the lawyer reading her will. "Yes, I remember bits and pieces. She left me the house." I thought for a beat, trying hard to unravel the difference between memories and dreams. "I'm not clear on details. My head is fuzzy and things come back in pieces."

"This is exactly why you need my help. Don't worry about anything. I'll take care of you. It's to be expected. You've been in a coma for twelve months." John nods, his expression unreadable.

I don't understand. "Twelve months? Are you sure?" I fall back into the pillow, closing my eyes. It can't be true. I must be dreaming.

"Yes, and you need to focus on your recovery and I'll get everything sorted."

I open my eyes, meeting his gaze. "There's nothing to sort out. What are you talking about?"

"Just trust me, Jessie." He leans in, his voice low and urgent. "I'm sending a lawyer with some papers for you to sign, and they'll explain everything." He sighs and straightens. "I have a client at four. I need to go but I'll be back tomorrow, if I can."

Trust is the last thing I feel toward him. As he leaves the room, with not so much as a peck on the cheek, I'm left with more questions than answers. I hear whispers in the passageway outside my door. Why are they whispering if they have nothing to hide? Doubt gnaws at me, and I can't shake the feeling that something is terribly wrong.

THREE

I'm awake early. Through the window I see the sun just rising above the horizon. Birds hop from branch to branch but I can't for the life of me remember what they're called. I close my eyes as the car wreck plays over and over in my mind like re-runs of an old movie. There's something on the edge of my conscious-ness, something very important that I can't grasp. It's the whisper you can't hear. The urgent warning I desperately need to know that's just out of my reach. I stare at my hands, trying to recreate the accident. I remember gripping the steering wheel and not being able to move it. Had something happened to the steering? Or perhaps the engine had failed? I close my eyes and I'm there inside my SUV, racing along the road in the darkness. Where are we going? Who is in the car with me? My girls are in the back seat but is John there? He says he wasn't but can I believe him? It's as if my life is cloaked in shadows—who is hiding in the corners of my memories and can I trust them?

Last night, after a dinner of chicken soup, Dolly explained why the doctors had put me into an induced coma for almost a year. I lost it for a time, screaming out for my daughters and demanding to see them. Each time I think about them, my stomach drops. Are they dead? Did I kill them? Why won't anyone tell me? Dolly just stared at me with her mouth in a tight thin line, saying nothing. I couldn't stop sobbing, and she stuck another needle into my drip. I don't recall anything after that. Lesson learned, I mustn't get upset or ask questions or I'm silenced and there's nothing I can do about it. I can't do anything or call anyone to help me. I'm too weak to get out of bed just yet.

"Good morning, Mrs. Harper." Dolly walks into the room carrying a tray which she places on the overbed table. "You're having something a little more substantial this morning. Your husband mentioned that you enjoy scrambled eggs and toast. The housekeeper made these; I hope they're to your liking. She will be in this morning to clean. Is there anything else you need?" She presses a button which raises me up to a sitting position and then slides the overbed table in front of me.

The meal looks delicious but I can't eat. I just want answers to my questions. Everything I ask is ignored so I must find another way to get information. "I would really like a cup of coffee. I'm over drinking water and orange juice." I lift my fork and taste the eggs. They are as good as they look. I smile at her. She stands by the bed, a pleasant expression on her face. Maybe she is a friend? "Have my parents been by or my brother?"

"No, but I'm sure they'll be by when the doctor clears you for visitors." Dolly adjusts my pillows. "Your husband is keeping everyone informed. You'll be teeming with visitors before you know it. Although I do know your mother is in Florida, your father is fine, and your brother is overseas at the moment. I believe he is due back soon."

So my parents are alive and well and Michael is off spending his inheritance in the south of France, no doubt. Interesting. I nod and continue eating. "She did talk about wanting to move to Florida. I hope she comes to see me soon."

"You can't rush things, Mrs. Harper." Dolly studies my face

and pats my shoulder in a friendly gesture. "The doctor insists you allow the memories to return naturally. You don't need any sudden shocks or bad memories creeping in and upsetting you. I'm not saying you have bad memories, but we all have things we'd rather forget and it's those things that cause the trouble." She smiles and nods at me. "I know it's unsettling but it's for your own good."

I raise my gaze to her before she leaves the room again. Maybe she has something interesting to chat about. "I guess I'll just wait then. What do you find to do all day?"

"Caring for you is a full-time job. I monitor your vital signs, administer your medication, and bathe you." Dolly gives me a long considering stare. "While you've been unconscious, I've given you physical therapy so that your legs will work when you decide to stand up. We'll try that soon. Once I remove the catheter you'll need to use the bathroom." She sighs. "I live in a room along the passageway. I have a monitor there where I can watch you in my downtime. I'm in constant communication on FaceTime with your doctor. He requires a daily update and I need to keep a diary on my computer of everything that happens during the day and upload it to his server."

I eat slowly, enjoying each mouthful. "It's very boring in here alone. Can you organize a TV for me or a radio? Do you know what happened to my phone?"

"Unfortunately I can't. We need to follow a certain protocol for someone that's just woken from a coma. Seeing things on TV that might upset you could put you back weeks in your recovery. The world has changed considerably in the last twelve months but you really don't need to worry about anything. Give it time and you will regain your memories." Dolly's mouth curls into a little smile. "I could get you some books from the library. The one here is extensive and I've been enjoying it immensely."

Why can't she ever give me a complete answer to anything I ask her? "Yes, I would like a book. A nice romance would be good, thank you. Can you tell me who else has been by to see me since I've been here?"

"Mrs. Harper and Amanda Blake came by to view the house." She must have caught my astonished expression. "Do you remember your mother-in-law?"

View the house? I have absolutely no memory of my mother-in-law but I nod and sip my juice. There's no need for Dolly to believe I have blanks in my memory and John's mother just happens to be one of them. "I do indeed, we're very close, but who is Amanda Blake?"

"The Realtor." Dolly smiles. "Mrs. Harper mentioned wanting to get the house valued now you're recovering, as you'd planned to sell it before the accident. Do you remember discussing the sale with your husband?"

I drop my lashes and stare at my plate. Sell my grandma's house?—Never. Stonebridge Manor has been in my family for generations. With ten bedrooms, there's room for everyone, and the cottages around the grounds offer privacy if necessary. I expected my parents to remain after my grandmother died but they'd decided it was my time to raise the twins in the family home and they purchased a house in Palm Springs. I wondered in that second if my mother had visited me. I lift my gaze back to Dolly and allow the lies to flow. "Yes, I believe I do. Have my parents been here to visit me?"

"I have no idea. I only took over three months ago." Dolly frowns. "It's unusual when coma patients are placed into palliative care, for them to get visitors. The family knows, they'll be notified of any change."

Say that again? I'd imagined John had brought me here to recover. A beautiful view over a rose garden, a tranquil setting to calm me while I gained strength. No wonder he'd looked so strained. He'd expected me to die. "So they weren't expecting me to regain consciousness?" I waved a hand as if brushing away any concern. "It must have been a difficult decision for

John to have the life support terminated. I remember discussing our feelings about placing a 'do not resuscitate' clause in our wills."

In fact, it was one I'd argued against, saying that all life was precious.

"Yes, I do recall that was in your case file." Dolly looks at me and seems at ease revealing the details. "Your life support was terminated after the first month, but you were obviously determined to live. Three months after the accident you were moved here and I'm the third nurse that your husband employed to care for you. I've been noticing an improvement of your brain function over the last few weeks; in fact it happened only days after I decreased the medication—on the instructions of your doctor, of course."

I lean forward, interested in what she is saying. "I can't understand the reason for keeping somebody drugged when they're in a coma. Unless it was an induced coma and I'm sure that wasn't the case, was it?"

"At first I believe it was, yes." Dolly lifts a tablet from a small table near the window, and scrolls through pages. "Yes, here it is. You had swelling on the brain and were placed in an induced coma to allow the swelling to recede. When the medication was reduced, apparently you seizured a few times and it was reintroduced and has been administered on lower levels over the last few days."

I force a smile on my lips. "Well, it's good that I made it through, isn't it? I'm sure I have you to thank for my excellent care."

"Thank you." Dolly pats my foot. "You relax now and I'll go and get you a cup of coffee."

I watch her go and my mind is in turmoil again. I can't believe what she just told me. I'd not only been placed in an induced coma but my husband allowed them to turn off the machine to let me die. When I didn't die, he sent me here with one nurse to care for me and this nurse wouldn't hesitate to reintroduce the drugs if instructed. Now he has plans to sell my house. *My* house! It's not *his* damn house. He doesn't own *my* house. He'll sell it over my dead body. Maybe that idea has already crossed his mind?

FOUR

11 MONTHS BEFORE THE ACCIDENT

Since confiding in Michael, the days blur together, and each one fills with a growing sense of uncertainty. The frequency of John's late nights and vague excuses have increased. Heartbreaking certainty has replaced my suspicions. I can't ignore the fact that something is wrong with our relationship. I need to know if he is having an affair. After dropping the girls at school, I've taken to driving by the building where John works. I park and walk into the exclusive Velvet Bean Café, a place I know he frequents for lunch, and sit and wait, passing my time nibbling on various pastries and drinking too much coffee. I never see him, not once and wonder what the hell I'm doing stalking my husband like some crazy person.

I haven't seen or spoken to Michael for weeks and when my phone chimes, seeing his name on the caller ID surprises me. "Hey stranger, how are you?"

"*Jessie, I saw John today.*" Michael's voice is low and urgent. "*He was having lunch with a woman at that new bistro downtown.*"

My heart skips a beat and then thunders in my chest. "Did you recognize her?"

"I'm not sure—maybe, but they seemed... close. It could be his lawyer, the new one, Rebecca Lawson." He clears his throat. *"It might have been innocent but I thought you should know."*

As I didn't know John had engaged a new lawyer, the information is gold. "How do you know her? I wasn't aware he had a new lawyer?" I walk around my immaculate family room, straightening photographs and picking up ornaments, not purchased for any other reason than they fit with the décor.

"She is a corporate lawyer and works with the firm." Michael keeps his voice low. *"I only know her by sight, she's a looker. Blonde, all legs, she's hard to miss. It wouldn't be the first time, would it?"*

I swallow bile as memories flood into my mind and make my stomach clench so hard I want to spew. I want to forget anything ever happened and that our marriage has always been perfect but during those early years, John was an arrogant ass. I shake my head. I can't deny it. I'd cried on Michael's shoulder too often at the time. I look at my wedding photo at the smiles and happiness we shared and sigh. "No, but that was years ago. He was young and it took him time to adjust into being married."

"You always make excuses for him." Michael blows out a long breath. *"He doesn't deserve your loyalty."*

My heart drops to the floor as a memory slides into my mind of being left alone at a party when I was eight months pregnant. I sat watching as my husband danced with another woman. The way he looked at her, got drinks for her, and hit on her in front of all our friends left a wound that will never heal. That night he didn't know I existed.

Those early days often involved other women. The one that haunts me is when he became close to a friend of mine, Daphne. We spent some happy times with her and her husband, Brad. They'd been trying to have a baby for five years and then, out of the blue, John started to take morning runs and would end up at her place. He openly told me about having breakfast with her and how she'd always butter his toast to the edges for him as if not doing so was a crime. I laughed it off but soon things changed dramatically. It wasn't long after I had the twins when I discovered she was pregnant. Soon after that, Daphne split with her husband and moved to a nice home in the next block. John was around there all the time, helping her change lightbulbs or whatever, and who do you figure was at the hospital when she had the baby? —John.

At the time, he suddenly didn't care about work and spent all his time with her, saying she needed him because Brad had left her. When I'd complain he'd shake his head and glare at me as if I'd become a monster. He insisted that Daphne was our friend and I was being possessive. The problem was, he spent more time with her than he did with me and the twins. I needed his support and felt ugly, tired, and lonely. His rejection confused me. I became depressed and wasn't coping with two demanding babies but he convinced me I was suffering from postpartum depression. Was he being a good friend as he claimed, or was the baby his?

My world came tumbling down when Daphne named the baby Renee. The name was the one John wanted for one of our twins and I'd rejected it, because it was the name of a bully at my school. Could the name Daphne had chosen been a coincidence? Tired and angry, I asked him if the baby was his and he denied it, saying he was only being a good friend. After that, he got angry if I ever brought up the subject, so I've just lived with the uncertainty. For me, the moment I saw the blue-eyed baby, the friendship with Daphne was over. Renee could have been one of my girls; the fact she was John's child was blatantly obvious. The next moment, without a word, she moved away. A few years later, I ran into her at the store and I came right out and asked the question. Do you know what her answer was?

"What does John say?"

What kind of answer is that? I walked away, dumbfounded, and now, with all that's happening, I ask myself, was I paranoid then too, because if I put the same question to any of my other friends now, will they react in a different way? Will they be shocked or at least deny it? All I can remember is the smirk on her face, like the cat that had gotten the cream. That was over five years ago and although a few of my acquaintances have tried to take him from me, he has, I believe, remained faithful, in body anyway—until now.

"Are you still there, Jessie?" Michael sounds anxious.

I stare at the picture of us at Christmas around the tree. We look so happy and I swallow hard. "If he doesn't want me anymore, why is he still living here?"

"Divorce wouldn't go down well with the company, especially on the grounds of infidelity." Michael pauses for a beat. *"It makes him look untrustworthy. You're a safe haven. The virtuous wife from an old money family; makes his clients respect and trust him."* He sighs. *"Look, Jessie, having lunch with the company lawyer doesn't mean he's having an affair. It might mean he's so busy it's the only time he had spare. This is why I'm not marrying for at least ten years. This job isn't really conducive to a good marriage. It's long hours to get results. I'll keep an eye on him, but I'll need to be careful, my job could be on the line if he finds out I've been snooping."*

"Thank you, Michael. Maybe I'm making too much out of all this." I chew on my bottom lip. "He does work hard and I knew it would be tougher this year since his promotion. I'm just lonely. Maybe I need to get a hobby?"

"That's my girl." Michael chuckles. *"I saw a flyer about art classes just yesterday in the window of the convenience store. You like art."*

I brighten my attitude; sounding like a death knell won't get me anywhere. "I'll look into it. Now get back to work or you'll be fired."

After hanging up, a mix of gratitude and dread surrounds me. I open my laptop and search for Rebecca Lawson. In seconds my page fills with images of a remarkably beautiful, confident, poised woman. She has a social media page, and when I open it, it's public, with images of her with congressmen, the mayor, and other dignitaries at various functions. I scan the images and my throat tightens as if I had a noose around my neck. She's at a function wearing a tight black dress, stilettoes and holding a glass of champagne, and standing right beside her in his tux, blue eyes dancing with amusement and his lips spread in a wide smile, is John. I scroll through the files and find more images of them together. Pain stabs at my heart. Indecision grips me and suddenly my beautiful home means nothing to me. It's an empty shell with all the happiness drained out.

FIVE
NOW

I walked today. Something that most people do without thinking but, for me, it took concentration, and the few steps to the bathroom were like walking a marathon. The shower taken seated on a plastic chair embarrassed me even though Dolly was very professional; being totally dependent on somebody else isn't something I relish. No one had styled my hair for a long time and once dried it hung past my shoulders like a silk scarf. The mirror in the bathroom had been covered and I questioned the reason why. Dolly informs me that I wasn't well enough to see myself. Have I turned into a monster? Is my face horribly scarred and the reason John didn't want to kiss me?

I need an excuse for Dolly to move away for a second. "I feel really sticky. Is there any powder I can use?"

"Yes, but you'll need to promise me you won't move if I go and get it." Dolly's eyes bore into me as if trying to read my mind.

I raise both eyebrows and laugh. "Where exactly do you figure I would go?"

The moment the bathroom door swings shut, I push to my feet, spread my legs apart to keep my balance, and wobble to the sink. I dig my nails into the paper covering the mirror and shred it to stare at my reflection. The face that looks back at me isn't damaged. I know I'm thin—being in a coma does that to people—but my eyes look bigger than ever before, set in a very slim face. I'm surprised I don't have any wrinkles. My forehead has always had a few but now it's smooth and so is my face. I actually look ten years younger although my body is thinner than I imagined. I toss my head, watching my hair shimmer. Not one white hair either and, for thirty-five, that makes me happy. I turn to one side and notice a scar on my shoulder. I don't recall ever hurting myself, but right now I don't care. The door opens and Dolly comes into the room, frowning at me. I look at her and smile. "The sight of me didn't make me hysterical after all, did it? I believe my face looks better than it did before the accident. Why is that, do you think?"

"From your file you suffered extensive facial injuries in the wreck." Dolly powders me all over like a baby. "During the reconstructive surgery, a cosmetic surgeon was involved. I'm glad you are happy with the results."

As she dresses me and I push my feet into pink silk slippers, I turn to look at her. "Do you know beforehand when my husband is coming to visit? The reason I'm asking is perhaps it would be nice if I wore a little makeup. He is acting like a stranger right now and seeing me looking normal might make things a little easier for him. I'm guessing he believes I'm an awakened corpse."

"Sometimes he calls, sometimes he just drops by." Dolly helps me to my feet and with one arm around my waist we head back to the bed. "Your mother-in-law is visiting today. I believe she is coming with the Realtor. She mentioned something about wanting to take measurements of something or another. She wasn't very specific."

Sweat trickles between my shoulder blades by the time I

reach the bed. "Okay, thanks. I'm hot; will you please turn up the air conditioning?"

"Oh, yes, and the lawyer is coming tomorrow at eleven o'clock." Dolly went to the control panel on the wall and then went back to the bathroom to clean up.

The door is open and I can see her collecting the towels and dropping them into a basket. "Do you know what his name is?"

"Her name is Rebecca Lawson." Dolly smiles at me. "I'll go and ask the housekeeper to bring your breakfast. It should be ready by now."

Rebecca Lawson. The name is like a whip lashing across my mind. She is the woman I see with John. I thought it was a twisted illusion from a jealous wife. Now images of her with John run helter-skelter through my brain. Why would he send a corporate lawyer to see me? The memories come back in a sickening thud. Why would he send the woman he escorts to business dinners to see his poor, sick wife? There are so many things I need to get straight. My brother Michael will help. Why hasn't he at least called? Maybe nobody has notified him.

My mind slips back to Rebecca Lawson. I recall the immaculate woman. Her good looks and stylish appearance had obviously caught my husband's eye and likely continues to do so. In the photographs they look the perfect pair. After the twins were born, John refused to take me to his business dinners, saying one of us needed to be home for the girls. More likely my constantly frazzled appearance, after caring for two very demanding babies, didn't fit with his image. My mind rushes from one scenario to another. What's been happening in the last year? Has John been seeing someone while I was dying in the hospital? Has he created a new life for himself with Rebecca Lawson? My heart squeezes so tight I gasp for breath. Maybe he wants me to sign divorce papers?

"Is something wrong?" Dolly's eagle eyes look at me suspiciously. "Have you remembered something?"

I shake my head and force a smile. "No, I was just thinking." I sighed. "You know, trying to remember but it's like walking in fog." I rub my belly. "I'm starving, you mentioned breakfast?"

"I'll head to the kitchen and Maria will be along soon. She'll bring it before she cleans the room." Dolly smoothed the blankets. "She's the housekeeper."

Whatever happened to Mrs. Jarvis? She loved her job and not having a family of her own, she'd looked on all of us as her surrogate family. I said nothing. I doubt if Dolly would even know about the old housekeeper. I know Mrs. Jarvis was left something in my grandmother's will so maybe she decided to leave and find a place of her own.

A short while later, Maria comes into the room with a tray. She is in her thirties, maybe, dark hair curled up in a bun and wearing a pristine housekeeper-type uniform. She gives me a shy nod and sets up the overbed table for me without saying a word.

When she comes back later, she collects the tray and then makes quite a performance of cleaning everything; wiping down surfaces and then pushing the vacuum cleaner around the room. Once she's done, she glances furtively out of the door, looking both ways along the passageway. She comes to the bedside and places a finger over her lips. I blink at her, not understanding what she wants, and then she presses a small envelope into my hand.

"This was handed to me by the gardener. He found it pinned to his shed." Maria glances toward the door. "Dolly told me to hold all your mail but this looks personal."

I squeeze her hand. "Thank you. I won't tell her."

As she leaves the room, I stare at the envelope, hesitant to open it. Hands trembling I tear it open. My name is typed and so is the message inside. My heart races at the warning.

Don't trust anyone.

SIX

Don't trust anyone.

Who sent me a warning? Is Maria involved? If so, has she overheard someone talking? A phone call? Why does she care? Jerked from my thoughts as footsteps sound in the passageway, I expect to see Dolly, but two women come into the room, arms filled with flowers and chocolates. I look from one to the other. They obviously know me but I don't recognize them. "Hello."

"Oh, don't tell me you don't recognize us; it would be such a pain." A woman about my age comes to the bed and places her gifts on the overbed table. "Have we aged terribly? It's me, darling, Sarah, and you know Laura—don't you?"

No, I don't. I look from one to the other, searching my mind. I recall having girlfriends but these two didn't fit the puzzle inside my head. I can't be thinking straight, and nod like an automaton. They exchange satisfied smiles complete with raised eyebrows as if I'm too feeble-minded to notice. With fake tans and casual dress, they do look like the crowd I hang out with. The uniform is usually cargo pants and floaty tops with designer sandals. The thing is, I don't know them, so what the heck do they want? Acting dumb seems the only way to find out because I have no idea what game they believe they're playing—or who sent them. "It's nice to see you again. I don't have any news; being in a coma does that to a person. What's been happening?"

"Oh well, we are on strict instructions not to speak about anything personal, like family or what happened to you." Sarah pulls up a chair and sits beside the bed. "You need to find your own memories but I can talk about old times. Do you remember when we played tennis and I tripped over that hunk of a tennis pro?"

I didn't but just nod and smile. That seems to make them happy.

"She did it on purpose. Remember the bet we had with her?" Laura frowns. "The first one to get his attention would make the others pay for lunch."

"Yeah, and he took me to lunch." Sarah chuckles. "I shouldn't laugh because Rose Sawyer told her husband and it got straight back to Steve. I needed to dance my way out of that one."

I look from one to the other, totally lost. These women are strangers and I have no idea what they're saying. I guess I'll make it up on the fly. "You didn't plan on having an affair with the tennis coach, did you? I mean, they do have notches on their belts."

"Why not?" Sarah grins. "We're not all as lucky as you, to have married a gorgeous man, who never ages a second. Looking at you, I'm starting to believe he's a vampire and has bitten you. Are you both eternally young? If so, bite me before it's too late."

Both women dissolve into laughter and I glare at Dolly as she enters the room. I hope she gets the message to throw the pair of loons out.

I look from one to the other. "If I was a vampire, maybe, but I don't have a hankering for blood just yet. In fact, I'm still very weak. I get tired so fast and my mother-in-law is coming over soon."

"The dragon lady?" Sarah wrinkles her nose. "She was at your house for a time. They packed all your things and gave them to Goodwill."

Stunned, I just stare at her. John threw out all my stuff? Why didn't he want to keep anything to remind him of me? Gathering my composure, I nod. "All my things? Well, that's good, I'll never fit into any of them now with my new sleek figure."

"Yes, he emptied the house, so I'm told. I did ask John's mother why he hadn't kept anything to remember you by." Sarah pats my hand. "She said he wanted to move on."

Heart thundering, I breathe deep and let it out slowly through my nose. I don't want them to know how much that's hurt me. "Well, he didn't, did he? My nurse tells me he comes by all the time and he was here yesterday and wants me better so I can go home. So someone is lying to cause trouble. Do you recall how long it was after the accident he got rid of my belongings?"

"I'm not sure." Laura looks uncomfortable and fidgets on her chair like a young kid needing the bathroom. "Maybe two weeks. We dropped by when we saw the Goodwill truck outside your house. I mean you'd spent so long making your home like a magazine spread and I guess we were nosy. Your mother-in-law said you were brain-dead." She rolled her eyes dramatically. "Obviously you're not." She turns over the book on the bedside table. "That cover reminds me of the play we did in high school. You remember that, don't you, Jessie? I played Juliet and you stood in the wings whispering my lines."

"Michael played Romeo." Sarah giggles. "He looked mighty fine in those tights."

No, I don't remember. These people are strangers and I don't recall being in a play with them or anyone else, and why would my brother be involved? Michael went to a different school—one for boys. My school was for girls, an exclusive private school. The chances that three students from the same school ended up living in the same gated community is very remote. What is going on here? Has my mind been damaged to such an extent I'm remembering a different reality? I shake my head. "That was a long time ago. I've a hard time recalling what I did yesterday."

"That's enough for today." Dolly steps forward. "Mrs. Harper needs to rest now."

"Okay." Sarah pats me on the arm. They must think I'm somebody's pet. "We'll be back soon."

Confused, I wait for them to leave and turn to Dolly, who is collecting the flowers. Would admitting I don't recognize them make things worse? Should I keep my mouth shut for now? Indecision is plaguing me of late and I'm usually so decisive. I remind myself that, although Dolly seems like a friend, she's under my doctor's orders and reports everything to him. The visitors have confused me and I need an excuse not to see them again. "Please make appointments in the future, and inform me, so I can get my head straight before they arrive." I wave a hand toward the door. "I don't want to see them again. They're too noisy and make my head ache."

"I figured seeing your friends would trigger nice memories." She gave me a long look as if trying to see the truth behind my shield. "But I can make a list for you to approve, if you prefer?"

Nodding, I push the chocolates away. "Thanks."

I need to talk to someone about my memory but can I really trust Dolly? I chew on my lip, not able to make a decision, but there isn't anyone else, and Dolly seems professional enough... maybe I can talk to her in confidence. Not getting back my memories might be significant and need treatment. I take a deep breath. Maybe if I bend the truth just a little. "You know, I hardly recognized them. I expect they've changed since

I last saw them but things are still a bit fuzzy. Is that a problem?"

"No, that's to be expected with head injuries." She smiles at me. "Don't worry, you're doing great."

I fall back into the pillows and the next moment Dolly returns with a cup of coffee and a slice of cherry pie. The aroma of freshly ground beans fills the room and mingles with the heady fragrance of the flowers. "Thank you."

"I'll ask Maria to bring some vases." Dolly indicates toward the door. "I'm taking a short break. Just press the buzzer if you need me."

I lie back, sipping the rich brew and running each year of school through my mind. Only significant memories remain, exam times and getting into trouble. Nowhere can I find any plays. I worked hard, enjoyed sports, and spent my spare time studying. There was a tennis coach at school, and I enjoyed playing the game. I still do and I'm good at it too and a member of the exclusive Grande Haven Tennis Club. I recall my other friends and their names but Sarah and Laura's faces don't fit into my memories anywhere. What if this is a permanent chunk of missing information? If so, what am I going to do?

SEVEN

10 MONTHS BEFORE THE ACCIDENT

At first, I decide not to confront John. It would be a terrible mistake if I'm wrong but the images of him with another woman keep playing on my mind. I know I'm stupid to be driving into the city to find the new bistro Michael had mentioned. City Lights Bistro is conveniently situated next to a parking garage. I wonder just how exclusive this restaurant is and if I'll need a reservation to get a table. As I push open the door, the first thing I notice is the high ceilings, above a sophisticated, stylish interior with elegant décor. Modern pendant lights above each table give muted and intimate light. The exposed brick walls are adorned with contemporary art, and large windows offer views of the bustling city streets.

The air is filled with the mouthwatering scents of gourmet dishes, freshly baked bread, and the delicate fragrance of herbs and spices. An attentive server waves me to a table with a crisp white tablecloth, fresh flowers, and polished silverware. He pulls out a plush seat, before handing me a menu. I scan it quickly and look at him. "Thank you. I'll order now. I'll have the lobster roll and coffee."

My attention is drawn to the busy street outside the

window. Vehicles stop and go in a constant stream of noise but, inside the restaurant, soft jazz plays in the background beneath the gentle hum of conversation, the clinking of glasses and silverware. I flick my gaze around the soft pastel-colored room. The clientele appears to be business professionals either in twos or small groups. It's a perfect place for a business meeting or an intimate meal. My meal arrives and tastes as good as it looks. It should be, as it costs more than a day's wages for most people.

I'm finishing a second cup of coffee when John's Lexus pulls up to the curb. He must be the only person on earth to get a parking place in Manhattan but then he does have an app on his phone. My heart starts racing and I'm not exactly sure what I should do. Dashing for the door is out of the question. I didn't expect to see him here; I just wanted to see where he wined and dined Rebecca Lawson. My gaze is fixed on the Lexus as John climbs out, walks around the hood, pulling his suit jacket down at the front, before opening the door for the lawyer. She is more gorgeous in real life than I had imagined. Her tailored business suit drips its designer label and her long legs rise from shoes only bought on Fifth Avenue. I could not possibly compete with someone like that. Despair at seeing them together grips me, but the answer to my question is there right before my eyes. Two thoughts flash through my mind: do I stand my ground, or run for the bathroom? My legs won't move and I'm stuck staring at the door as if mesmerized but they walk right past me and my stomach drops to my boots at the way John rests one hand in the small of her back.

The concierge greets him by name and they are led to a discreet table in direct eyeline to me. John is so involved with his conversation that he doesn't notice me at first, but as he lowers the menu after ordering, his eyes lock on me across the room. He frowns, waits for the server to retreat, leans in to speak to Rebecca, and then stands and walks toward me.

The woman gives me a cursory once-over and then dives

into a briefcase. Have I unnerved her or is that the look of a woman caught with someone else's husband? I look good today. Being married to John means that I have designer clothes as well and the appointment with the beauty parlor earlier gives me the confidence to smile at him. "So this is where you bring her— how fitting?" I reach for my coffee, trying hard to stop my hand trembling.

"Don't make a scene, Jessie. You know I'd never cheat on you." He bends to kiss me on the cheek and then slips into the chair beside me. "What are you doing here?"

As his cologne washes over me, so deliciously familiar it squeezes my heart, I notice the flush creeping up his neck and stare into his concerned deep blue eyes. I believe it's the first time I've ever seen my husband off guard. "Michael told me about this place. I was in town so I decided to see if it stood up to its reputation. I didn't expect to see you here. More importantly, what are you doing here with Miss World? Are you trading up to a new model? I don't blame you, John, I must be at least two years past my best by date."

"Why do you always react like this when you see me interact with women? I work with women, represent women, and I'd say at least twenty-five percent of my meetings happen over lunch." John shrugs. "It's really the only time I have to spare. Right now is an important time for me to shine at the firm. One of the old partners is retiring and I'm in line for the position, so I don't want to be seen dropping the ball." He sighs and reaches for my hand. "I know I'm away from home too much, but if I can get the partnership, I'll be able to delegate some of my work to others. It's something I've worked for my entire life." His hand is warm and dry over mine as he strokes his thumb across my suddenly sensitive flesh. "Miss World, as you call her, is the firm's corporate lawyer and we're negotiating contracts."

Words spill out of my mouth before I can stop them. "I do

recognize her actually. She came up in a black-tie event on social media a month or so ago. You were with her then as well, sipping champagne instead of being home with your family." I held up a hand to stop his retort. "Oh, I understand. It's strictly business, isn't it, John?" I laugh at the absurdity but see a shadow cross his eyes. "Don't worry, I won't make a scene but you best get back to Miss World. I do believe I'm making her jealous." I cup his chin and then run a finger down the front of his shirt. "At least now I know why you won't wear your wedding ring." I twiddle my fingers at him. "Run along now or you'll be missed." I signal to the server for my check but before I can drop the credit card onto the plate, John pushes to his feet.

"Please put my wife's tab on my account." He gives me a long look. "I'll be late home tonight. Don't hold dinner for me." Without another word he turns and walks away.

Holding my head high, I walk from the bistro and somehow make it back to my SUV. All I can see is John with Rebecca Lawson. If she works at the firm he would be in contact with her daily. How can I ever compete with that? She sees him more than I do. Michael suggested I confront John but I don't believe he'd approve of my actions in the bistro. I pushed John into a corner. His usual way of arguing is to throw his arms into the air and pace up and down. He always wins because I'm afraid of losing him, but this time, he knew his lame excuse wouldn't satisfy me, so he punishes me. You see, saying he won't be home for dinner, in John speak, means he won't be home at all.

EIGHT

NOW

Trepidation at the thought of seeing my mother-in-law fills me, especially after the note Maria had pressed into my hand, which insisted I don't trust anyone. I wait in hope of seeing Maria come by to pick up the lunch tray. When Dolly left to eat her own lunch, she mentioned running a few errands. I'm alone and helpless. The sound of footsteps from the passageway and the squeak of wheels brings Maria at last. I beckon her closer, touch her arm, and smile at her. "Thank you for giving me the note but can you tell me who it is I'm not supposed to trust? You understand I've been in a coma and my head is a little muddled at the moment, so any help you could give me would be very much appreciated."

"I don't know who sent it. It was given to one of the gardeners over a week ago. I kept it safe for you but I hear things and I see things." Maria looks at her hands and then lifts her eyes to me. "They speak about you as if you're dead and what they plan to do with everything that is yours."

That much I'd deduced but hearing it is a reality check. They're all vultures, circling my body. I shake my head, sad that it's come to this. "I know they took my things from the house and gave them to Goodwill, so I guess they didn't believe I would survive the accident."

"No, not the things from the other house." Maria looks furtively around her. "This house. The members of your family have plans for this house and they don't want you to know about them."

I swallow hard. Could my entire family be plotting against me? Is there no one I can trust? I consider what she said for a moment. "Do you answer the phone?"

"Yes, on occasion, but Dolly insists I leave it to her." Maria frowns. "She says she's concerned that I would give out information to the wrong people. As you probably know, being from a prominent family means the media is interested in how you're doing. The family don't give them any information whatsoever."

Suddenly frightened to ask the question, I take a deep breath. "Has my mother or father called the house and has anyone mentioned my kids?"

"Not to my knowledge." She picks up the tray and shakes her head sadly. "I only answer the phone if Dolly is out which isn't very often as everything is delivered to the house. Most times she gets calls here on her cell. If that happens in my presence she leaves the room."

I need to keep her here for a few more moments. I have more questions to ask her. "How many times has my husband been here to visit me?"

"Many times." Maria's eyes keep flicking toward the door.

My heart thunders in my chest. "And my children? How many times has he brought them to see me?"

"I have never seen your children." Maria shakes her head. "I'm sorry, Mrs. Harper, there's nothing else I can tell you."

My heart sinks to my boots. It's as if my girls don't exist. I fight back tears as overwhelming grief of not knowing if they are dead or alive floods over me. I need to see my twins. Their angelic faces fill my head and then vanish. Suddenly I can't remember what they look like. Panic grips me and I hear the alarm in Maria's voice drifting into my head.

"Mrs. Harper. Are you okay?" She gives me a little shake. "I didn't mean to upset you. I'm so sorry."

Forcing back tears, I reach for a glass of water and take a few sips. "I'm okay. I just miss my girls." As suddenly as they'd gone, the twins' faces fill my mind and I suck in a deep breath in relief. After not recognizing my best friends, and now forgetting my girls' faces, I figure my head is more muddled than I realize. I reach out and touch Maria's arm. "Keep listening. After hearing my husband gave away all my things to Goodwill, I believe anything is possible. I'm a woman of means and will reward you for any information you bring me, the moment I'm up and about."

The sound of footsteps in the hallway has Maria scuttling away and the next moment Dolly walks in the room. I look at her. Maria hadn't cautioned me against Dolly, so maybe I could trust her. "I would love a cup of coffee the next time you're brewing a fresh pot. Lunch seems like a year ago. I do believe I'm regaining my appetite."

"That's good to know." Dolly removes packets of drugs from a paper sack and places them in a dresser drawer. "You're doing very well with your walking now and as soon as your mother-in-law leaves, I'd like you up and about. The more you walk the stronger you'll become." She goes back to the hallway and returns pushing a walker—the type older people use after a hip operation. "You can use this and it will help you get mobile again. If you get tired, it has a seat so you can rest for a time."

Voices in the passageway catch my attention and almost at once the doorway fills with the robust figure and stone face of Eloise Harper. I recognize her at once and a chill runs through me at the sight of her arrogant expression. She doesn't believe I'm good enough for her son. I went into the marriage penniless and the only things that make life easier between us are my family name, my grandmother's house, and the fortune that goes with it. Although when I married John I had no idea my grandmother would leave the house and fortune to me. I always imagined she would leave it to my mother as she'd raised us in the house but it was my grandmother's intention for me to raise the twins on the estate.

"There you are, Jessie. It's good to see you." Eloise peers at me over the top of her glasses and waves her hand absently at the woman beside her. "This is Amanda Blake, the Realtor we've engaged. We'll be here taking some measurements. Don't worry, we won't get in your way."

I stare at her, uncomprehending. "It's nice to see you too, Eloise. Before you rush off, would you mind explaining exactly what you are doing in *my* house?"

"Oh, didn't John tell you?" A flash of annoyance crosses Eloise's face. "He plans to convert the house into either prestigious luxury apartments or a hotel. On this estate, Amanda informs me they would command millions. The same would be for an exclusive hotel for the rich and famous. Can you imagine the marketing on something like that? 'Spend your vacation in the lap of luxury at Stonebridge Manor.'" She writes in the air as if seeing a billboard.

I shudder and give her a direct stare. Desperation gnaws at my belly. "I'm sure he'll get around to it. Eloise, how are the girls? You've seen them, haven't you?"

"I..." Her mouth puckers like a cat's anus and she turns on her heel and rushes from the room.

"You know the doctor's instructions." Dolly comes to the bedside and pulls back the blankets. "All personal information is to be placed on pause for a week or so to allow you to get your bearings. With regard to your children and the accident. In here —" she taps her temple "—you know what happened, and when the memories come back, the doctor will take it from there.

Okay? So don't keep asking. Just let the memories come back naturally."

I stare at her. "I remember them fine, so why the secrets?"

"Okay." Dolly's face holds an unreadable expression. "Tell me what happened three days before the accident, or even what happened on the night of the accident? Let's start with where were you heading?"

I stare into a space between her head and the wall. The dream comes back in flashes but the space where memories of that night should be is empty. Nothing. "I remember taking them to dance classes on Tuesday night, was it on the way home?"

"You wrecked the SUV on a Friday." Dolly sighs. "That's all I can tell you and no doubt the doctor will haul me over hot coals because I mentioned it. He'll be by to see you in two weeks. By then he'll be able to suggest if you need any further assistance. Maybe hypnotism."

I turn my gaze on her. "Why do they need to get to the bottom of it?" I swallow the fear rising in my throat and restricting my breathing. "Did I do something bad? Did I cause the wreck? Is that why I can't see my girls?"

"There you go getting upset again and all I did was tell you the day you wrecked the car." Dolly crosses her arms over her chest. "This isn't helping. I don't want to sedate you but I will if you don't calm down."

Sucking in a deep breath, my mind is working overtime. I can't allow her to see. "I'm fine. I just need to get out of this room for a time. It's getting like a prison cell."

"Okay." Dolly relaxes and nods. "Exercise is good; just don't overdo."

I slip from the bed and push my feet into the slippers. My legs wobble as if I can't take my own weight. I stand there, swaying like a tree in a storm, before I get my balance. Taking tiny hesitant steps, I push the walker around the room. I admit it's helping me. "I'll try and make it to the library."

"That's good." Dolly smiles at me. "I'll make up your bed. It's much easier to change the linen without you in it."

So slowly, inch by agonizing inch, I shuffle my way along the passageway. I bypass the library and head straight for the family room. I need to see my twins even if they're in a photograph. I push my way inside and the walker slows on the plush carpet. I'm exhausted but take in the familiar room. It's old-style luxury, padded chairs and a long sofa. The other furniture purchased in the 1930s is very much the art deco style, all straight lines and angles. I've spent many happy hours in this room, and recall coming downstairs to find brightly colored gifts under the Christmas tree. My grandmother's spaniel, whose name was Arthur, used to bark and go crazy when we tore the paper off the gifts. You see Grandmother would tell him not to touch them. I had a beautiful childhood growing up in this house and as I inhale the familiar scents of woodsmoke and pine cones, I can almost catch the lingering smell of my grandmother's lily of the valley perfume.

I go to the sideboard and stare at the silver-framed photographs set out on a lace doily. It's handmade and was brought home after my grandmother's honeymoon in Europe. I take a walk down memory lane as I recall the stories behind the images. I run a finger over the photographs of my grandmother's wedding, my mother's wedding. My brother's and my christenings are there alongside the photographs of my wedding. I touch John's handsome face, and my love for him glows inside me. He is still the best-looking man I've ever seen. I move on, anticipation of seeing the girls' faces again races my heart. I stare in disbelief—the christening photographs and birthday images of my twins have vanished. In fact, all the photographs I remember of my parents with my girls, from Christmas and birthdays, that filled the sideboard are missing. I desperately search the room, and open drawers, but there's no trace of them.

Trembling, I push the walker to the fireplace and stare at the mantle. Pictures of my grandfather in his military uniform and one of my grandmother holding my mother as a baby. All the other photographs I know should be here are missing. I shake my head. Bewilderment grips me in a rush of uncertainty. I recall giving birth, seeing John's happy face as he held the newborns in his arms. Watching them walk, taking them to school for the first time. It is all inside my head. Why did Dolly tell me that I must remember what happened to the girls and my parents? A vivid image of John's cold and remote expression when I'd asked him about the girls fills my mind. The love that I'd basked in for seven years is gone. Is what happened too horrible to face? Was the accident my fault and I've blocked it out? Does everyone believe I wrecked the car on purpose—that I tried to kill myself and my kids? Suddenly the remoteness from the love of my heart makes terrible sense and I can't for the life of me remember what really happened. God help me.

The day my grandmother died still haunts me. The stroke that eventually took her life had also taken her speech. It's so clear. I can see every second in my mind.

I'm standing beside the bed in those final moments, and I know she is trying to communicate with me. I remain there alone as dark shadows creep across the hospital grounds. The family has come and gone during the day, the doctors informing them that the end is coming but they can't put a time on it. John has stood beside me for an hour or so, his solid strength and warm press of his hand comforting. The scene is dreamlike as if it can't possibly be happening. I grasp my grandmother's winkled hand. It reminds me of a chicken's foot. Fine boned, with dark veins that extend to her pathetically thin arms. Only her eyes appear to be normal. "Blink twice if you're trying to tell me something, Grandma."

When she blinks twice my heart races. "Is it about someone in the family?"

She blinks twice again. I grab the family photograph beside the bed and hold it in front of her. Slowly I point to each person and say their name. I watch her closely and when I come to my father, she blinks twice. "Is there something you need to tell me about him?"

She blinks twice.

I rack my brain trying to recall our last conversation. It had been almost a month ago. My grandmother was in her nineties and she'd been going through family documents, kept in the safe at Stonebridge Manor. She'd wanted to tidy things up and put her affairs in order. Had she discovered something? "Does this involve anyone else in the family?"

She blinks twice.

I run my finger over each of the people in the photograph and when my finger lands on an image of me, she blinks twice. "There's something not right between my father and me?"

She blinks twice.

I love my dad. He's always been there for me. I couldn't imagine anything not right between us. I need more information and stare at my grandmother but she closes her eyes. A tear trickles down her cheek and the machine beside her squeals in alarm. Footsteps come thundering down the passageway. I step to one side as two nurses check her vital signs.

"She's gone." One of the nurses looks at me, her gaze sympathetic. "Do you want more time with her?"

Emotion rolls over me and I shake my head. "No, she's not here any longer. I need to tell my family."

* * *

One week later, I stand in the grand entrance of Stonebridge Manor and inhale the air thick with the scent of old wood and memories. My grandmother's funeral was a somber affair with everyone dressed in black under the cold gray sky, my mother's constant sobs the only sound in the heavy silence following the eulogy. I'm back at the manor for the reading of the will. Only the immediate family assemble for the reading. I'm surprised when John arrives and comes to my side, muttering that he'd managed to grab a couple of hours from work to be here. I thank him and he straightens beside me, nodding to the family members. Flawlessly presented, his expensive suit makes my two-thousand-dollar, simple black dress look like a rag. I look at him and my stomach flutters as it always does when he's around. I'm not sure what happened between him and Rebecca Lawson but after going missing for three days he arrived home and carried on as if nothing had happened. Had I won this round? I smile to myself as I glance up at him. I crave his attention but he avoids my gaze and checks his Rolex. Every minute is money to him, or should I say, second. Does he want to save our marriage or is it the fortune I might inherit that has kept him with me? "I'm not sure if I should be dreading this or be excited."

"I'm sure we will find out soon enough." John clears his throat. "I just wish he'd get on and be done with it."

At last, the lawyer, David Collins, an amiable man with a sharp gaze, ushers the family into the office. Tension fills the room and the hair on the back of my neck stands to attention as I sit in the semicircle of chairs set before a desk littered with documents. Collins takes his seat across the desk and perches a pair of half-moon glasses on the tip of his nose. His gaze sweeps the group and no one utters a word. The silence is deafening.

"Until certain conditions are met, the residuary bequest, which includes the remainder of the estate after all bequests have been distributed, will be withheld. I'll speak to anyone concerned after I conclude today." Collins peers over his glasses. "I can only deal with the specific bequests, which are particular items or a specific amount of money given to a beneficiary."

I sit, staring at him, noticing that a long hair on a mole on his cheek swishes back and forth like a whip as he talks. He reads the document. My mother receives a substantial sum of money, as does my brother; I'd believed everything would go to him. The housekeeper receives a nice retirement fund and I get nothing. I'm dumbfounded.

"Who gets the manor?" My mother leans forward in her chair. "It's our family home, we have a right to know."

"You will be informed in due course, but right now, I'm legally bound not to discuss the terms of the will to anyone other than the beneficiaries." Collins looks at her. "For those of you who received specific amounts, I'll be contacting all beneficiaries to obtain bank details for the transfer of funds."

Shellshocked, I stand, ready to leave, and stagger a little and then John has his hand on my back. I look at him as we walk into the hallway and his face is totally blank. "I must say I'm a little disappointed."

"That's life. It's full of disappointments." John indicates with his chin as the family heads toward a smorgasbord set up in another room. "You go along and get something to eat. You're sheet white. I can't stay. I need to get back to the office." He kisses me on the cheek.

I grab the front of his shirt and press my lips to his. To my surprise he responds but then gently sets me away. I know he hates public shows of affection but the hallway is empty. He smooths the front of his shirt and I see a twinkle in his eyes that has been missing for a long time. I smile at him. "Thank you for coming. I really needed your support today."

"That's what husbands do, isn't it?" He gives me a brilliant smile and then turns and heads toward the open front door.

I watch him go, realizing I'm totally dependent on him again. Before my grandmother died this was the case but there'd always been an uncertainty about who would inherit the estate or part of it. I'm surprised she left me nothing. Perhaps this is why he'd ended the affair with Rebecca Lawson, because if the multimillion-dollar estate had fallen into my hands he'd want to handle the money. Maybe hearing I'd received nothing had made him smile? He believes I have no option but to stay with him and endure his affairs. He has no idea that if I decide to leave him my brother has offered to care for me and the girls. I cross my arms over my chest as his Lexus sprays the driveway with gravel as he speeds away. "I have more options than you realize, John."

I turn as Collins appears in the door to the study. "Won't you join us for refreshments?"

"I'm not finished yet. Do you mind taking a seat in the study for a moment?" Mr. Collins stands to one side to allow me to enter and shuts the door behind me.

The unmistakable click of a lock disturbs me. All of a sudden, the study seems darker than before with the only light coming from a single lamp on the desk. Heart pounding, I spin around to face him. "Is that necessary?"

"Yes, it is. What I have to say to you is confidential." Collins sits down behind the desk. "Please sit down, Jessie. Your grandmother left everything to you—the manor and a substantial sum of money but there's a condition."

A chill runs down my spine. "Condition? What condition?"

"You know your grandmother was passionate about the estate remaining in the Stonebridge family. You must agree to this clause to inherit. This means you need to rewrite your will, ensuring your brother Michael, and not John, inherits the estate if you die or become incompetent."

Dumbfounded, I look at him. "My children have the Stonebridge blood. I can't believe that my grandmother would make me write my girls out of my will."

"It's complicated." Collins runs a hand down his face and stares at me as if not wanting to divulge any more information. "If you leave the estate to your children, and they haven't attained the age of twenty-five as stipulated in your grandmother's will, your husband John will be in control of the estate. Your grandmother did not want him involved and added this stipulation just before she died. Apparently, your brother had spoken to her recently and mentioned John's infidelity."

Michael ran to Grandma about John? I can't believe it. Why would he do such a thing? I stare at the table, trying to get my mind around a solution. "So I can't mention my children in the will? Can we get around the stipulation by saying that Michael is the trustee of the estate until they are twenty-five years old?"

"No, the estate must be left entirely to Michael, if he is of sound mind and doesn't have a criminal conviction." He sighs. "You can stipulate that if Michael dies without an heir, or doesn't meet the original criteria, the estate goes to your children, once they attain the age of twenty-five." Peering over the top of his glasses, he rests his elbows on the table and towers his fingers. "Once the will has gone through probate, I will speak to Michael's attorney and request he makes that provision in his will. If he refuses, we'll move to plan B."

I lift my chin, resolute to ensure my girls are well provided for. "I don't have a problem with Michael inheriting the estate but if it belongs to me now, I owe it to my children's future to include them in my will. I must insist that my children are included if I agree. I'm assuming you already have a codicil for me to sign?"

"I do and will make the changes to your will. I must caution you not to reveal the specific details of your inheritance before the estate is legally in your hands because it leaves it open to a challenge from your brother. I don't represent him so need to protect your interests." He gives me a long, concerned look. "You do realize that any profit you make from the proceeds of your inheritance, including investments, belong to you. If you filter them into a trust fund for your children, no one can challenge their entitlement."

I could easily go to John for financial advice, but until I'm sure our marriage is solid, finding someone else outside the family will be crucial. I nod. "Yes, that sounds like a plan. I know you've worked for Grandma in this office. Do you have everything here to produce the copies I need to sign? I'd like to get all the legalities finalized if possible."

"Indeed I do." He opens his laptop. "I'll come and get you, when I finalize everything. Just remember, it's in your best interest not to divulge the terms of the will. Your grandmother was very clear about this." He hands me a letter. "This is for you. I hope it explains everything."

I take the letter and open the door. A shadow moves and I hear soft footfalls. Was somebody listening at the door? I hurry along the passageway, in the direction of the library, expecting to see Maria or one of the family but only the murmur of voices comes from the family room. Did I imagine someone was there? With so many things happening at the same time, it's becoming difficult to cope. It seems I can't believe my own eyes right now. I slip inside the library, closing the door behind me. It's a safe place and I can relax here. I sniff the envelope. It smells like my grandmother. A wave of misery washes over me. I miss her and the house is empty without her. I turn on the light above a favorite chair, sit down, and tear open the envelope. My grandmother's distinctive handwriting blurs as my eyes fill with tears.

My dearest Jessie, if you are reading this, Grandma has left the building. There are things I wanted to tell you but I've kept them secret for your protection as well as your mother's. The truth can destroy lives but you're strong enough to rise above it. The information I discovered is buried within the walls of Stonebridge Manor. Find it, and you will understand everything. The only piece of advice, I can offer you, is don't believe what people tell you, not even those closest to you. Grandma.

What truth? I peer around the room. I spent many happy times reading in front of the fire but suddenly the security has vanished. The shadows play tricks with my mind and dark corners seem to whisper secrets I can't quite hear. If I can't tell anyone, what can I do? As sure as hell I can't discover the secrets on my own. Why hadn't she been more specific? I look around and swallow hard as the walls seem to close in around me. What truth must I know about? Is something terribly wrong in my family? If so, why did Grandma believe I can fix it?

I stuff the letter into my purse and hurry out of the door. I need to speak to Mom, but if the news will hurt her, maybe not. I must tell her the estate is mine now—or will be once probate goes through but that could take a year or so. Dad has run the estate since my grandfather died but if this involves him, he's off the list as well. No wonder he didn't come to the reading of the will. Maybe he believed his secret would come out?

I can't involve John—not yet—but I need to speak to him and tell him about my inheritance. Today it was nice to enjoy the old connection we once had and it was so good to lean on him, even for a while. He'll be happy for me—won't he? I check my watch. He'll be driving back to the office but my call will go through to his phone via the Bluetooth on the Lexus. I make the call.

"Jessie? Is there a problem? I'm ten minutes out from the office." John sounds annoyed.

I hear a giggle in the background. "Are you alone? What I need to say is confidential concerning what we attended today."

He says nothing. I hear a grunt as if John is trying hard to stifle someone close by. Then a female voice comes through the line like a dagger straight to my heart.

"This is Rebecca Lawson. I'm John's attorney. I'm sure anything you need to say, you can say in front of me."

I slump against the wall as every ounce of fight drains away in a wave of misery. Suddenly, everything fell into place. I'm such a fool to believe it was all over between them. The sparkle in John's eyes hadn't been for me; he'd planned on meeting Rebecca or had her holed up somewhere waiting for him. I'm sure my heart is bleeding and the cut is so deep nothing will heal it. I straighten as anger takes over. How dare he treat me like this? I must turn the tables on the self-confident woman and fast. I might be a simple housewife but I know how to play the game. I've had plenty of practice since marrying John. I chuckle as if hearing her voice amuses me. "Oh, Ms. Lawson. I remember you. John has mentioned you work for him. I'm afraid this is much too personal to share with *you*." I take a breath and my hands are shaking. "John, are you there?"

"I'm still here, Jessie."

"We'll talk later tonight, darling. This exciting news is for your ears only." I disconnect and lean against the wall, panting.

What is he going to say, when he discovers I'm wealthier than he is? Will he try and control my estate and maybe syphon most of it into his accounts? I don't exactly trust him right now. What he'll never know is that his chances of getting his hands on one cent of it, if I'm dead or alive, is zero.

TEN

It's Michael who finds me in the passageway. His concerned gaze moves over me, and I'm enveloped in one of his bear hugs. It's as if he can feel my pain. I gently push him away. "You're crushing my dress."

"You look like a puppy in a pet store window." He pushes a strand of hair behind my ear and bends to look directly into my eyes. "What's happened? Is it John again? I can't believe he actually came to listen to the reading of the will without Rebecca. Every time I see them at work they are joined at the hip. Although, I did hear mention that they were working on something big."

I chew on my bottom lip, not sure what to tell him. I have no proof that John is having an affair although everything I've discovered points to it and I'm too much of a coward to face him again and demand the truth. I know, I'm just being a doormat and I should hate him—but I don't. He's always been the love of my life and this way at least I get to see him, even if it's for fleeting minutes. I can hope he gets bored with her and comes back to me. You see, admitting my husband is attracted to someone else is like saying I'm not worthy. It's a terrible feeling.

It's a useless horrible stomach-dropping sensation to lose someone you love so very much to another. To know he only lives in your house because he's obligated to, is soul destroying. I give my head a little shake. I can't admit the truth to him. "It's not that, Michael. I'm a little shocked is all."

I take a deep breath. Explaining without giving details is going to be difficult and as much as I want to, I can't explain about Grandma's letter. What she'd written could be the ramblings of an old lady. For some reason she'd stopped trusting my dad. Maybe she was becoming unbalanced toward the end? I need to tell Michael about the will. *I might as well get it over with.* "Grandma left the estate to me." I look at his strange expression. I'm not sure if he's surprised or devastated. "I'm so sorry, Michael, I thought it would go to you or Mom."

"I know." Michael slips his arm around my shoulders and pulls me close. "Grandma called me, six months or so before she had the stroke. She had a bee in her bonnet about some of the investments Dad had made on her behalf. She said she trusted me to look over them and give her an opinion. I honestly couldn't find anything wrong apart from the fact that Dad had shares in many of the same companies." He sucks in a breath. "She asked me point blank if I would invest in my client's portfolios. Of course, I said no, it isn't something our firm encourages." He sighs. "Maybe I tipped over a wasp's nest by saying that because soon after, she told Dad it was time he retired and she wanted someone younger to take over her accounts. She called me in again, and I assumed she wanted me to handle the investments but she'd already engaged another stockbroker."

I shake my head slowly not understanding what this had to do with the will. "I know Dad retired but what does this have to do with the will?"

"Grandma told me she'd be leaving the estate to you, with me as the spare if anything happened to you before she died." Michael chuckles. "Trust me, I really don't want the burden of this place hanging round my neck. It's a huge responsibility and the taxes are incredible, as you'll likely discover. I'm more than happy with my share. I'm very good at my job and that will be double by the end of next year." He gives me a side eye. "You don't have to worry about Mom either, she is over the moon with her inheritance. Another thing is we'll get the money right away. Collins has a ton of work to do before the estate is actually transferred into your name. It's a long process. It will likely take twelve months." He gives me a squeeze. "So don't do anything stupid in the meantime. Trust me, I don't want the responsibility of this place. Although John would be in his element, he could run the investments with one hand tied behind his back and being the part owner of Stonebridge Manor will push him to the top of the social ladder. I'm guessing it will even put a smile on his mother's face."

I shake my head. "No doubt. Maybe then he'll be able to afford a better business lawyer than Rebecca Lawson." I snort with laughter. "In fact, I'll insist on it."

* * *

It's five after ten, and I hear a key in the lock as I sit in the kitchen nursing a cup of coffee as I peruse the stack of paperwork the lawyer gave me. The money the company estate generates over twelve months is mind-blowing. I can't get my mind around the figures. To think my great, great, grandfather managed to get through the Great Depression and subsequent family members played the dangers of the stock market to this extent and came out on top is beyond my comprehension. I can't honestly believe why my grandmother left it to me. I have no idea what to do with it.

I glance up as John walks into the kitchen. With not a hair out of place, it's hard to believe he's been working at all but I do notice he's changed his tie. "New tie."

"You're very observant." He loosens the tie and slipped it from around his neck, dangling it between two fingers. "I forgot to wear my tiepin today and it dropped in my coffee. I could hardly speak to a client with half a latte on my silk tie, could I?" He stares at the documents on the table with a frown. "What's all this?"

I take the first page of the will, listing all my entitlements, and hand it to him. The codicil with the new provisions listed I kept hidden under a pile of documents. "Of course nothing becomes legally mine until the will has passed probate." I wave to the other pile of documents. "All this is about assets and investments—all the financial stuff, I know nothing about." I wave the last tax return at him. "I had no idea my grandmother's estate made so much money."

"Your father did mention the extent of her portfolio." John's eyebrows lift as he scans the tax return. "You do understand he didn't handle the portfolio alone? He managed the direct finances of the estate but he engaged a brokerage firm for all this. No one person could possibly be responsible for Stonebridge Manor's assets." He shrugs. "They were doing so well. I don't understand why your grandmother insisted the estate be handled by another firm. From these figures your father had placed everything in secure hands." He picks up a document. "They're in the hands of Legacy Securities. It's a big firm. I'll look over the portfolio and see how they're doing but it's up to you if you want me to handle them? It would mean even more money in our pockets, I'd earn commission." He gave her a slow smile. "Bringing an account this size to the firm would push me right to the top."

That's the first time he's ever called his income, "our" money. Funny, how suddenly when I get money it's "ours." I stand and pour him a cup of coffee. "Are you hungry? I know it's late but I can throw together something."

"No, I'm good, thank you." John meets my gaze. "I had a

business dinner. It's happening more and more now I've been promoted. I'm afraid it means I won't be home as much for dinner. Give me time and I'll delegate some of the work but just now, I can only go with the flow."

You're never home now. I sigh. "It must be difficult for Ms. Lawson to keep her figure when she's out to lunch and dinner all the time." I reach over and pluck a long blonde hair from his shoulder. "She's left her calling card I see."

"Well, at least she's easy on the eye." John smiles at me. "I could have been saddled with an old crone. Usually the clients are so taken by her, I can drive a good deal."

I shake my head, trying to cover my feelings. Am I making too much of the fact he finds his workmate attractive? "I'm sure she does but I believe she's overstepping the mark when she tries to come between a husband and wife's private conversation. What was she doing in your car anyway?"

"I explained I had a client waiting and it's usual for me to take her to the meetings as she's the firm's corporate lawyer." John blows out a long, frustrated breath. "I'd arranged to drop by to collect her, so I could spend more time with you. What was so important? You're not pregnant, are you? I'm not sure I could cope with a baby right now."

I look at him in disbelief. How could that even be possible? "Then you don't have to worry, do you? I called to tell you I'd inherited over one hundred million dollars and thought it would make you happy." I stand, pick up my phone, and head for the stairs. "I'm going to take a shower. Don't forget to lock up."

"Jessie." John follows me to the steps. "You can't keep pushing me away like this."

I turn and look down at him, unable to believe my ears. He's trying to turn everything around as usual and blame me for our marriage problems. Is this sudden change of heart due to the fact I've inherited the Stonebridge estate? "I'm not driving you away, John. Not at all. I just find it difficult to get close to you when you come home smelling of perfume."

"I'll take a shower and send my suit to the dry cleaners in the morning." He rubs his chin thoughtfully. "I'm not sure why that would be upsetting to you, Jessie. I apologize I hadn't noticed. I guess sharing an office with someone all day, who lathers herself in fragrance, means some would transfer to me. As you said, she is an employee. I will insist she refrains from wearing fragrance inside my office."

I giggle at the absurdity. "Honestly, John, you can't do that. She's an attorney and knows the rights of people in the workplace. It's like telling her she can't wear the short skirt and stiletto heels. The times when the boss was allowed to insist on personal details is over. I would suggest you don't get so close to her, especially as she's leaving hairs on your collar."

"How do you know it's not one of yours?" John starts up the stairs toward me.

I laugh and wave a hand in the air. "Because I'm a natural blonde. We women know the difference." I head into the bathroom and lock the door, confident I'd scored my first point. I just wish it would make me feel better. The uncertainty of my husband spending so much time with a single woman he admires is festering into a wound my heart can't survive.

ELEVEN

NOW

I've got to get away. I'm sure someone is trying to drive me insane. I know there were photographs of my girls in the family room. I can remember clearly going to buy the frames and giving them to Grandma to put on her dresser. Is this all part of a plan to take Stonebridge Manor away from me? It takes an effort for me to push the walker through the door and along the passageway to the library. This is one of my favorite rooms in the house. As a child, I would sit on my grandma's lap in the big comfy chair beside the fire and listen to her read stories. Now, as I cross the threshold, cold seeps into my bones, like a warning from the past. I scan the room although nothing has changed; it's empty because Grandma is no longer there to greet me with a smile.

I'm exhausted and sweat runs down between my shoulder blades but I'm determined to keep going. Pushing the walker is easier in this room as the floors are highly polished wood, the color of rich mahogany from many years of polishing. The walker makes a soft rumbling sound with a slight squeak as I make my way to the bookshelves and the line of photo albums. All have been leatherbound and have the years on the spine in gold lettering. I look along the line and select the books from the date my daughters were born. I place them on the seat of my walker and take them to a desk beneath a window overlooking the rose garden.

I start turning the pages slowly and speed up when all the photographs I know should be there are missing. I scream in frustration, throwing one of the books against the wall. It crashes to the ground, spilling photographs across the floor. I tear at my hair, trying to force my muddled brain to think straight. The photographs should be there. Where are they?

Footsteps thunder along the passageway and Dolly arrives, a frown wrinkling her brow. I need an excuse or she'll figure I'm losing it again and stick me with a needle. "I was looking at the photo albums, trying to recall everyone's names. I became frustrated. I'm sorry, I shouldn't have lost my temper."

"I thought you may have fallen. I'm glad you're okay." Dolly bends to pick up the photographs and albums splayed out across the floor.

It's all too much for me and I'm swaying like a snake getting ready to strike. "I couldn't find the book from the year before I had the accident. I wanted to see if everyone came to the manor for Christmas as always."

"I'll see if I can find it for you. "Dolly scans the line of books. She plucks one out of the center and brings it over to me places it on the desk. "No wonder you couldn't find it, it was out of order."

My fingers tremble as I open each page. I recognize everyone in the shots but my girls are missing. I flick through the pages and then stop, going back and forth. The immaculately bound volume has pages missing. They'd been cleverly removed using a knife but the rough edge of where a page should be, remains. I look at Dolly. "See? There's a page missing from here."

"I don't think so." Dolly runs a finger down the inside of the book against the spine. "It looks perfectly fine to me." She turns the pages back and forth, examining them. "Maybe it's your eyes playing tricks on you. It can happen after you've been in a coma so don't worry about it too much. I bet when you come back in a couple of weeks and look at these again, they'll all look perfectly normal to you too."

Without warning, a flash of a memory strikes me like lightning. I'm reading a letter from my grandmother and she is telling me not to believe anything anyone says. *"In a couple of weeks they'll all be perfectly normal to you too."* Does that mean they plan to replace the books, so I have no proof that the page ever existed? And who is *they*? Is Dolly a part of a conspiracy against me for whatever reason—or am I losing my mind?

I can't breathe in this room and want to throw open the windows to allow the scent from the rose garden to come inside. Confusion is closing in on me from every direction. I can't rely on my recollections but I need them to get well. My gaze follows Dolly as she replaces the books on the bookshelf and then turns to face me. I force myself to smile, likely looking more deranged than agreeable. "I'm going to try and make it to the office." I step out into the passageway and Dolly follows close behind. "It seems so quiet without my mom and dad here. They always had the radio or TV blaring. Did you know they purchased a condo in Florida? After my grandmother died, they only remained here for a few months so that my father could tie up some loose ends. The probate on the will was still going through." I stare at her, suddenly realizing that was almost a year ago. "That must have been just before my accident. The IRS got involved and needed to be satisfied before it was settled. It was fortunate the staff wasn't fired and they continued to be paid during that phase or the grass would be up to the eaves."

"I don't know anything about the business of the estate, Mrs. Harper." Dolly looks confused. "I believe my paycheck comes from your husband."

My husband? Surprised, I head slowly toward the office. The thought of John being in control of my investments turns my stomach. Why is it upsetting me? It would be natural for me to ask him to manage the investments. He is excellent at his job and makes people millions but something in the back of my mind is nagging at me. As I walk into the office and look around, I try to expand on the memory of reading a note from my grandmother. What did it say? Nothing else filters into my mind apart from recalling opening an envelope and seeing my grandmother's distinct writing on the page.

I stand at the door, surveying the scene before me. It is much the same as when my father left it. As the financial adviser to my grandmother, he handled the estate finances for a year before my grandmother died. I recall my father being upset that she'd suddenly decided to take the estate out of his hands. She'd employed a brokerage firm to take over her portfolio and a financial advisory company to take over the running of the estate but complained they were too sterile and had planned to move again. Then she'd suffered a stroke and I can only assume that John stepped in and took over. I can't for the life of me remember the few months before the accident. It's coming back so slowly, like a dripping tap of knowledge.

As I look out of the window at a gardener, trimming the bushes, another memory comes to the front. Stonebridge Manor has an estate manager, Mr. Barns, who keeps everything running smoothly inside and out. My grandmother gave him a substantial annual budget to take all the stress and worry away from her. Shouldn't Dolly be paid by Mr. Barns? She is, after all, an employee? I notice Dolly is still hovering behind me, no doubt waiting for me to have another outburst. I turn to look at her over one shoulder. "Do you know if Mr. Barns is still working here? He has a small cottage in the grounds."

"The estate manager?" Dolly nods, observing me with interest. "Yes, he is still here. He came by for a cup of coffee when I first arrived and informed me that your husband insisted he fire many of the staff. He wasn't very pleased about it as the estate is extremely large and needs all the gardeners and other staff to maintain it. The main cutback was in the house staff. We have a cleaner who comes in twice a week, mainly to help with the washing, then there's only me and Maria. As you know, I have a bedroom along the passageway but close to the sunroom where you are and cameras and monitors were brought in so I could watch you twenty-four hours a day. I did ask for a relief nurse, but your husband didn't think it was necessary for a coma patient with do-not-resuscitate instructions." She sighs. "Not that I'm complaining but I need to go out sometimes and Maria isn't qualified to care for you."

I look at her and nod. "As soon as I am back on my feet, I will make sure that Mr. Barns has all the staff he needs. I really need to know about my financial situation but I can't imagine John has managed to abscond with my entire inheritance in twelve months."

I walk into the office and stare at the shelves. One part of my head is telling me something is significant about these shelves. Curiosity drags at me and I push my walker toward them. As I browse them, my head aches and my heart thumps in my chest. Am I having a panic attack, and if so, why? What happened in this room to frighten me? What is significant about the shelves?

I try to push the feeling away. Another flashback grips me in an instant of information. I'm flipping through the pages of a notebook. I screw up my eyes, trying to remember. I can see Grandma's writing but the words all swim together as if they're falling off the page. I tried to reach for the memory again but it's gone. Was it really a memory or just an injured mind playing tricks on me?

Waiting for probate to go through is like spending time at the dentist's office. I'm expecting something bad to happen although everyone is telling me it will be okay. I've been back to Stonebridge Manor once a week for the last three weeks and I find myself here again today. I started my search in my grandmother's bedroom, spending hours going meticulously through every nook and cranny. I even looked under the mattress, to find some type of a clue to what the letter referred to. Everything of value is inside one of the two safes in the house but until probate goes through, I am unable to obtain the combination from the lawyer to open them. I did however manage to question him on the contents. I insisted I wasn't concerned about any valuables, but my grandmother's letter had mentioned perhaps a diary or some personal letters, I needed to read. There are a number of documents inside both safes but mostly involve the running of the estate. Everything else would be included in an audit, to enable estate taxes to be paid. My grandmother was very intelligent and she would have known any access to the safes would be limited once she died, so I could only imagine she'd left something within the walls of

Stonebridge Manor that held the information I was looking for. The family room has yielded nothing of interest and I'd move my way to the office, picking up and reading every scrap of paper including old newspapers I'd found tied up with string in a corner.

Grandma didn't trust computers and refused to have a mobile phone. For me that is a relief more than a problem for I have absolutely no idea how to break into a computer. I walk into the library and throw open all the blinds. Behind me, the housekeeper, Mrs. Jarvis, is watching me in dismay. I turn to look at her. "Will you please open some of the windows? It's very stuffy in here."

I start on the desk, methodically going through everything but find nothing of interest. I turn and look at the rows of books on the shelves behind me. If Grandma hid something there, it will take me a year to find it. I stand in the middle of the room, slowly scanning each shelf one by one, looking for anything out of place. My attention moves to the bottom shelf over in the corner closest to the window, and I notice a small brown abnormality. I head for it and ease out a leather-bound diary. It is squeezed between an encyclopedia and the end of the bookshelf. I flick it open and fist punch the air when I see my grandma's handwriting flowing across the pages. I've found it!

I sit at the small desk and a mixture of excitement and trepidation crawls over me. The diary covers five years; it will take me an age to read. I consider my options. If my grandmother had discovered something terrible, wouldn't she have told somebody? Why did she wait until she was on her deathbed before she mentioned it? So whatever happened must have happened in the last year. I find the page and start moving forward. Most things are day-to-day entries. Local gossip and her meetings with the book club. As I get to six months before her stroke, the writing changes and becomes a little erratic.

I was in the office today when the phone rang. It was a woman looking for Joseph. She spoke to me as if I were his secretary. He wasn't here and I offered to take a message. She said her daughter, Emily, had taken a fall from a swing and was in the E.R. She insisted the moment he walked in the door he was to come at once. I was too dumbfounded to question her, and if she hadn't used the name Joseph, I would have considered she'd called the wrong number but I did make a note of the phone number. I might be old but I'm not stupid.

I ran my finger over the phone number; it was local. I move back to the pages, unable to believe what I was reading.

When Joseph arrived, I followed him into the office and closed the door behind us. I asked him if he'd been cheating on Dawn. The look he gave me terrified me. I thought he might strike me. When he asked me why I would ask him such a question, I told him about the message and he sprung to his feet and ran out of the door.

I stare at the writing and swallow hard. My father had cheated on my mother. Had she suffered the same way as I am suffering now? Are we both just doormats for men to wipe their feet on? I believed my parents were happy. They are planning to buy a condo in Miami, or so I thought. I stare at the wall, trying to get my thoughts into order. Come to think of it, it's my mother who wants to buy the condo. My father prefers life here, and he'd mentioned, during a discussion in front of the family, that starting afresh at their time of life was a mistake as all their friends were here in Connecticut. I move my attention back to the diary.

After seeing the guilt written all over his face, I couldn't stand the sight of him any longer. The next time he walked through the door I told him he was fired. I said I would tell the family that he'd decided to retire. Again I saw the anger in his face and it chilled me to the bone. I asked for more information from him about the child but he refused, saying I was a confused old lady who was just trying to make trouble. Today I called a private detective and he came to see me right away. I gave him the details and the phone number plus a substantial retainer. I needed to know everything about Joseph's affair and daughter. His name is Jim McCloud and his number is in my phone book.

I read fast, turning the pages, sifting through the day-to-day entries until I find more information about my father.

I have all the information I need to confront him. Photographs of him with a woman young enough to be his daughter and a child. He has set them up in an apartment in Manhattan no less, using funds syphoned from my estate. He is coming later today. I will insist he tells Dawn and I'll tell him, he'll never get another cent from me.

Horrified, I can't believe my eyes. My loving caring father has another family he's kept secret for years. Shocked, I read it again and note this entry was written two days before the letter she'd given to the lawyer. I turn the page to find it empty. I push both hands through my hair and my stomach twists. There must be more information. I turn the pages back and forth but find nothing. My heart races at the implications. That last entry was written the day Grandma suffered the stroke.

THIRTEEN

NOW

I woke this morning with dread gripping my stomach. Rebecca Lawson is coming today and I'm sitting here in a hospital gown. John hasn't supplied me with any real clothes, or as much as a pot of moisturizer. I sent Maria to my mother's old bathroom in the hope of finding some cosmetics but it's apparently empty. She was, however, able to supply me with a few of my grandmother's toiletries. She did indeed have expensive tastes, and the creams and lotions rescued from her bedroom are of the finest quality with many of the boxes unopened. Maria also found a gown and brought it to me fresh from the dryer.

I sit in bed, trying to make myself look as reasonable as possible, which isn't really easy. I'm very thin and my legs stick out from under the short nightie like twigs. The gown will cover them and at least match the silk slippers I've been wearing. There's no way I'm going to speak to Ms. Lawson in bed. I will be in the office when she arrives. One thing is for darn sure, she won't see me using the walker. It takes me time to climb from the bed and grasp the walker. I look out of the window. The sight of the rose garden calms me. I insist on having the windows open. It's the middle of summer, and the smell from the garden is wonderful.

I walk around the room and the only thing I recognize are the drapes. They are the same throughout the house. Heavy and old fashioned, they look like something that would be found in an old English mansion. I recall the walls had many pictures on them. The one of a bunch of daffodils in a glass vase which I'd always admired is missing; in fact at least four pictures are missing. I push my way along the passageway to view the other reception rooms. I find it difficult to open the heavy wooden doors. I must be weaker than I imagine as they were easy to open even as a child. I'm surprised to discover the furniture is covered with dust covers, and in this room all the pictures have been removed from the walls and even the figurines and the clock I recall above the mantle are missing. Perhaps they have been put in storage for safekeeping? Each room I come to is the same and it makes me feel so disoriented. In my mind I was only in here a few days ago, for the reading of my grandmother's will. But it wasn't a few days ago, was it? Halloween decorations were going up all over the night I had the accident. In my recurring dream, I see a jack-o'-lantern hanging from the tree my SUV is heading for.

I lean against the walker, trying to remember that night. How much of it is a dream and how much of it is the truth? I recall reading about people who have experienced bad things and never recall what happened. It said their brains are telling their minds that if they know the truth it will damage them in some way. What was the name, ah yes, anterograde amnesia. I smile; parts of my memory seem fine. If that's what's wrong with me, I wonder how I can unlock the secrets. Finding out what happened before the accident is the key. I recall Grandma's diary and the revelations about my father. Maybe reading it will jog a few brain cells into action. I shuffle to the library and time does a shift. I'm suddenly back hunting down the diary but this time I know exactly where I hid it. I go to the bookshelf and edge my way toward the window to the very last book. I remember pushing the diary back into its hiding place and run my fingers between the small space. It's gone.

I turn on the lamp and peer into the tiny space. No one knew where I'd hidden it and I'd never told a soul. I stare at the bookcase and swallow hard. Is this another delusion? Am I imagining a past that never happened? Who would know? If I ask anyone, I just get generic answers. I must discover the truth of the lost days before the wreck. It's the only way I'll get to know about the girls. Where are they? They won't even tell me if they're dead or alive. Tears sting the backs of my eyes and I'm trembling as I try and gain control. I can't allow Dolly to see me upset. Or she'll sedate me again. Getting well is the only way to discover the truth.

"Mrs. Harper. A vehicle has pulled into the driveway. I believe it's the lawyer. Should I organize refreshments?" Maria hurries to my side and examines my face. "Are you well?"

I smile at her. "Just sad to see the rooms covered up is all. I'll wait for her in the office. Please bring refreshments."

I push the horrid walker slowly along the passageway and into the office. The desk has been cleared at my request and the books placed neatly in a pile on a table. I push the walker behind one of the thick tapestry drapes, and taking slow wobbly steps, make it to the office chair. I'm hot and exhausted but when I sit down, calm comes over me as I smell a hint of my father's cigars. Everyone hates them but for me the smell means he is close by and not working away in his office in Manhattan. All the men in my family worked there, in flash glass and steel buildings with wide windows. Another memory that's clear, I can recall every inch of John's office. His leather topped table was much like this but this one has been here through generations. I run my fingers over leather oiled by many hands, and wish I'd known all of my family who'd sat in this very chair.

Rebecca Lawson breezes in the door. She's wearing a black business suit with a blue silk blouse, and I can't help but notice how short her skirt is, but as John considers her attractive, I guess it's all part of her work ethic. Her black stiletto heels had heralded her arrival, and sounded like the clip-clopping of a horse. That thought is in my mind as she drops a folder on my desk in front of me and holds out a hand. I imagine she must have forgotten the day I discovered her with my husband in the bistro having lunch.

"Rebecca Lawson." She shakes my hand. "How are you? I believe John mentioned I'd be coming to see you about signing some papers. I'm the corporate lawyer working at Titan Brokerage with John."

I stiffen as I look down at her wrist and the world tips sideways. She's wearing the same Tiffany bracelet John gave me on our wedding day. I consciously look down at my wrist. I've never removed it and it was the first thing I noticed missing when I woke from the coma. Is she wearing *my* bracelet? If so, did John give it to her? Did he remove it from my cold wrist believing I was dying to give to his girlfriend? My lunch curdles in my stomach and bile rushes up the back of my throat. I glance at Maria who is hovering in the doorway, looking at me. "Maria, would you please bring coffee and maybe some cookies or whatever you have on hand?"

I turn my attention back to Ms. Lawson. "Yes, Mr. Harper did mention that you would be dropping by. Exactly what is it my husband wants me to sign and why does he need a lawyer to deliver it rather than bring it himself?"

"He is exceptionally busy and believed you might need professional guidance before signing the documents." She sits down and crosses her legs before reaching for the folder. The sheer stockings make a swishing sound as she moves her legs and dangles one patent leather shoe. "These are power of attorney documents. When you sign these the estate will be released into John's hands to act on your behalf. Since the will went through probate after you had your wreck, it has been in limbo for the last twelve months while we wait for your recovery. You are in no fit state to run the business. John... ah, Mr. Harper believed now that you are awake you would be only too happy for him to take over the stress of running the estate."

I recall quite clearly what my lawyer told me about Michael informing Grandma that John had been unfaithful. Her wishes were that he never gained control of the estate and here is this woman trying to insist I sign over everything I own to him. I don't even look at the paperwork in front of me but clasp my hands over it and look her straight in the eye. "Are you a specialist in coma patients, Ms. Lawson?"

"I'm not exactly sure what you mean, Mrs. Harper." Ms. Lawson looks down her nose at me, a folder clutched against her chest.

I smile at her. "I mean, how are you qualified to determine if I'm fit enough to run the estate? Do you believe that my mental capacity is diminished in any way? I may not be fit enough to do the New York City Marathon this year but I'm quite capable of running the estate."

"I believe you have a long road to recovery. John mentioned that you weren't yourself yet and are having memory problems. I don't know you well enough to offer an opinion on your mental state, I'm afraid." Ms. Lawson raises both eyebrows, making her smooth forehead pucker. "I'm sure, John only wants to make life easier for you."

The bracelet on her wrist glitters in the light as she touches her hair and I don't even have my wedding ring. They'd stripped everything from my body, everything I cared about. I swallow hard, trying to sound logical and of sound mind. "I will speak to my lawyer about this because as far as I'm aware as the executor of my grandmother's will, it's his responsibility for the continuity of the business and the estate." I watch her blink a few times as if not quite understanding why I don't fall into line. "Please inform my husband that I would appreciate it if he would contact me immediately. As you can see, I'm still wearing hospital robes and I've been awake for almost a week. I need my clothes and I also require my phone, laptop, and a line of credit, without delay."

I want to toss the papers at her face but I keep my temper in check. Any show of aggression would likely add another week to anyone telling me about my girls. "I will be sure to contact my lawyer about this matter and get back to you once I've listened to his advice. Thank you for dropping by."

"I'll relay your message to John." She stands and pushes a folder back into a briefcase and click-clacks back along the passageway.

I open the drawer and take out my grandmother's phone book. I easily find Mr. Collins' phone number. I lift the receiver on the landline but the phone is dead. I shake my head in disbelief and slowly replace it in the cradle. The small address book I slip into the pocket of my gown, and press my hand on it, feeling the smooth leather under my fingertips. It's such a small item to cling to but with everything going weird, I need a constant, and that little book proves I had a past, with people and loved ones. Determined to make a call, I get up slowly and retrieve my walker from behind the drapes. I'm getting stronger but by the time I reach the library my body is coated with sweat as if I'd just finished a vigorous exercise routine. I push my way to the phone and lift the receiver. Nothing.

I know I must get back to the office before I'm missed, and stagger into the room just as footsteps and the rolling wheels of a cart rumble over the wooden floors. Panting, I drop into the chair. Why aren't the phones working? I rest my elbows on the table and push my hands into my hair, holding my head and thinking back over the last few confusing days. I'd spoken to Maria about answering the phone and the line was working then or she'd have mentioned it. What is happening? I feel as if I've been cut off from the world. Or did I imagine speaking to Maria? Concern and frustration grip me; I feel trapped as if I'm being kept prisoner. Why would my husband be doing this to me? I'm sure Mr. Collins doesn't know I'm being treated like this; I bet no one has told him I'm awake. At least he has my best interests at stake? I can trust him... can't I?

I look up as Maria arrives pushing a cart with afternoon tea. The rich aroma of coffee fills the room along with the delicious smell of cinnamon buns. I wave her inside. "Close the door and sit with me. I'd like to ask you a few questions." I wait for her to sit. "Have a cup of coffee with me... I need to speak to someone, I'm so very lonely. If Dolly asks you, I beg you to keep my confidence and just tell her I asked about your family."

"What is it you need to know?" Maria sits and then pulls the cart toward her and pours coffee into two white porcelain cups with red roses on the side. They are part of my grandmother's distinctive dining set.

I reach for a cinnamon bun and place it on one of the matching plates, licking the sugary syrup from my fingers. "Do you have a working phone in the kitchen? How many phones do you figure are in the house?"

"Yes, I do." Maria places a cup of coffee in front of me. "There is another by the front door, the library, here in the office, and all the bedrooms and reception rooms, I believe."

I take a bite of the cinnamon bun and the rich flavor moves over my taste buds in a sugary delight. Since waking, everything I've eaten seems to be enhanced in flavor. I lean back in the office chair, making it creak. "When you get the chance, could you walk around and check to see if they're working? This phone doesn't work and neither does the one in the library and I need to get in contact with my lawyer about the paperwork that Ms. Lawson delivered." I search her face but all I see is interested honesty. "Would you be able to call him for me from the kitchen?"

"Wouldn't that be something Dolly should do for you?" Maria held her cup above the saucer, her brown eyes wide. My request was obviously making her nervous.

I take the small book from my robe pocket and write down the number for Mr. Collins' office. "You know about the note and have kept it secret so I know I can trust you." It's essential I speak to my lawyer. I don't know who disconnected the phones to prevent me from using them. So far Dolly has been very honest with me and I trust her but I know she stops me doing things for my own good. She might consider speaking to my lawyer too stressful but I need to get this paperwork sorted. I push the number toward her across the desk. "Please help me."

"Okay." Maria glances behind her and then nods. "I don't believe it would hurt for me to call your lawyer." She quickly pushes the slip of paper into her pocket. "I'm sure he is fully aware of your condition and what he is allowed to say to you during your recovery."

The familiar squeaky sound of Dolly's shoes comes from the passageway. I indicate to the door and laugh. I need to make up something fast to cover our conversation. "I've always loved Halloween. My brother and I would feel so sick afterward. In our neighborhood they would literally fill our buckets with candy and we'd spend all night sorting it out and eating most of it."

"Oh, there you are, Maria." Dolly looms at the door. "I hope you're not tiring Mrs. Harper. It's time for her to take a rest."

I look at Dolly and smile. "Why don't you join us? We were just chatting about all the antics that we did as kids during Halloween."

"Did you get the paperwork signed?" Dolly leans against the doorframe, eyeing me like a hawk. "I didn't notice Ms. Lawson's vehicle when I returned from the store."

It's none of Dolly's business. The paperwork is between me and John. I find it quite strange that she's trying to insert herself into my personal affairs. I decide to change the subject. "Do you know if any of my personal effects were brought here to the house after I left the hospital? I'm missing my wedding ring and a bracelet. I haven't removed either since I married John. I feel naked without them. They hold very special sentimental value."

"Nothing came with you from the hospital apart from the drugs required to keep you going." Dolly sighs as if it's all too much trouble. "I contacted your husband, to inform him that you were breaking out of the coma. He brought the slippers with him. He mentioned that he didn't believe your shoe size would have changed but he could see you'd lost weight."

I look at her; she doesn't appear to be trying to mislead me. "Did he bring me clothes?"

"He did mention that none of your clothes would fit you any longer." Dolly lifts one shoulder in a half shrug. "Men are all the same; he wouldn't have a clue what size to buy you. Maybe I'll grab a tape measure, so you can give him your measurements and tell him to buy you some clothes."

I return her smile. "If I had a laptop and my credit card, I could go online and buy my own clothes. John is a very busy man." I lift my chin. "Did you know this phone isn't working? I wanted to ask my lawyer, Mr. Collins, a question about the paperwork and now everything is delayed until I see him again. Has he mentioned dropping by, do you know?"

"The phone was working fine yesterday; I used it myself." Dolly gives me a quizzical stare. "I haven't spoken to your lawyer. Next time Mr. Harper drops by, maybe you should speak to him. I don't believe you should worry yourself over the documents. I doubt there's any need to call a lawyer. Your husband would be only doing things in your best interest. You trust him, don't you?"

You mean, my cheating husband who is trying to get control of my inheritance? I bit down hard on the inside of my cheek to prevent the words leaking out of my mouth and force my lips into a smile. "Of course I do. It was a simple question is all. It's nothing you need to be concerned about." I yawn and cover my mouth. "I'm exhausted. I figure I'll go and rest."

I stand, seeing the satisfied look on Dolly's face. She is the person I must convince all is well. My girls' faces drift into my mind, I can almost hear them laughing as they play. I ache to see them. I need to be sure they're okay. Gathering myself from a pain that's tearing me apart, as if I'm mourning them, I straighten and push my walker back to my prison. I can only hope Maria contacts my lawyer and then maybe I'll get some answers.

FOURTEEN

7 MONTHS BEFORE THE ACCIDENT

Now I'm aware of my father's secret family many things start making sense. I'd been informed like everyone else in the family that my father had decided to retire. Following this he'd taken a long vacation leaving my mother behind. I can't remember him ever taking a vacation without my mother so this alone gives me pause for thought. I don't want to blindly tell my mother that my father has been deceiving her for years without absolute proof. At the time, I'd asked her about Dad's long vacation and she'd given the excuse that he planned a guided hunting trip and killing things wasn't something she enjoyed. I'd mulled all this over before revisiting the diary again. I searched for any overlooked details or hidden messages. I'd hoped to find cryptic notes or codes that pointed to more details but after searching for ages, I found absolutely nothing.

As my parents are still officially living in the manor, it's difficult for me to search the house. Although since the reading of the will it is technically my house, snooping around makes me feel like an intruder but I have no choice. I need the information that my grandma obtained from the private detective. I hate lying to my mother but I need an excuse. On my drive here this morning I ran a number of things through my mind. I believe I have my stories straight now, and as I walk into the kitchen and inhale the familiar scents of home, I'm surprised to see my mother dressed in a neat suit, pulling on gloves. She's going out and the house is empty. I can't believe my luck. "Are you going somewhere?"

"Just for a few days." My mother smiles at me and it reaches her eyes. "I'm going to Florida to look at some condos. It's been a dream of mine for so many years but I felt obliged to remain here with your grandmother to make sure that she was well looked after in her later years." She waves a hand in the air. "Now she's gone there's nothing holding me here. I know you will be able to visit me and I you. It's less than three hours' flight from here you know."

I look at her, dumbfounded. "But you'll be all on your own. You don't have any friends there."

"Oh, but I do." My mother laughs and bends to peck me on the cheek. "It has become the go-to place for burned-out stock-brokers. Many from my tennis club live there now, and this is one of the main reasons I'm going. As I'm getting older, I'm running out of friends." She runs a hand down my arm and gives me a little squeeze. "I'm not deserting you, Jessie, I'm just living what life I have left to the full. I hope you'll do the same when you're my age."

A horn sounds from outside, and my mother picks up her purse and hurries toward the door grabbing a suitcase on wheels as she goes by.

"That will be my cab to the airport. I'll see you in a few days."

I follow her to the front door and stand in the lingering scent of her perfume as she drives away. Now, I have at least three days to search the house from top to bottom. I need help and speak to Mrs. Jarvis. She has been employed as the housekeeper for my grandmother for as long as I can remember. She agreed to stay on until I found a replacement for her.

I walk back into the kitchen and find Mrs. Jarvis has already poured me a cup of coffee and has cookies set out on a plate. It's the same each time I arrive. She treats me as if I'm still at school. I sit down at the table and watch her tidying up the kitchen. I can think of no other way than plunging right in and asking her outright. "You were with my grandmother for a very long time and I'm sure you were friends. Can you recall any places my grandmother may have hidden private documents apart from the safe? I've already asked Mr. Collins about the contents of the safe and what I'm looking for isn't inside. My grandmother left me a letter and asked me to search for the information she scattered around the house. It's personal things that she only wanted me to see."

"In the few months before she had her stroke she rarely went out of the library or her bedroom and sometimes the family room." Mrs. Jarvis wipes her hands on a towel and sits at the table. For a woman in her late sixties, she is remarkably preserved and could pass for forty. Although she does complain about her knees from time to time. Her blue eyes move to me. "I would imagine if there was something hidden it would be in those rooms. I don't know of any particular hiding places but if she didn't intend your parents to find them, I'm sure she wouldn't have left them lying around so we have to assume they're in a very good hiding place."

Nodding, I look at her kind face. "While I'm drinking my coffee can you tell me a little about my grandmother's last days?" I took a sip of the rich brew and peered at her over the top of the rim. "I'm aware that she had a disagreement with my father and he retired soon after. I don't really care how people spin it but I know from the letter she left me that she actually fired him."

"I do recall a mighty argument in the office, the day before she suffered the stroke." Mrs. Jarvis shakes her head slowly. "As you know, I usually walk outside if anyone starts arguing in the house. It's not my place to get involved. I walked into the rose garden and I could still hear your father screaming at her."

Suddenly I'm very interested. "Do you remember what he said? Don't worry because my grandmother set out many things in a letter to me and I'm just trying to get to the bottom of it." I give her a direct stare. What the heck? If she knows something, she needs to know I'm aware of the truth. "I believe she discovered evidence to prove my father was having an affair. I don't want to say anything to my mother about this until I know the truth. What I need to find is the information given to Grandma by the private detective she hired. Do you have any clues where she might have hidden those documents?"

"I believe she gave them to your father." Mrs. Jarvis leans forward in the chair, her face serious. "When I cleaned the office early the next morning, there was evidence of shredded photographs in the trash. I didn't think of it again at the time because that was the morning I found your grandmother desperately ill. I'd taken her breakfast to her room as usual and found her on the floor in front of the hearth. The paramedics believed that she had been there all night."

Tears well in my eyes at the thought of my grandmother lying on the floor alone, unable to move. It must have been a terribly long night. I pull a tissue from my purse and dab at my eyes. The terrible thought that my own father had caused the death of my grandmother by screaming and yelling at a woman in her late nineties circled in my mind. I look at Mrs. Jarvis. "Do you recall where my mother was that day?"

"Yes, that would be the weekly meeting of her quilting club." Mrs. Jarvis nods sagely. "She wasn't here for dinner that evening, and your father ordered pizza, because he didn't like what your grandmother had chosen for supper."

I think for a beat and then look at her. "So my grandmother

would have chosen the time she knew my mother would be away to confront my father about his affair?"

"If what you are saying is correct, then yes, I would say that's right." Mrs. Jarvis frowns and wags a finger at me. "Don't you go jumping to conclusions now. You know as well as I do that your grandmother was a little strange toward the end. She would often forget what she was doing. I've seen her stand at the refrigerator for ages trying to remember why she was there."

I frown. Admittedly I hadn't seen much of my grandmother in the last six months before she had the stroke. "Maybe you'd better explain. If you have any doubt she'd become confused before she had the stroke, it might be significant."

"Let me see. It was happening more frequently toward the end." Mrs. Jarvis stares into space. "There was a time she figured she saw your grandfather in the garden and ran out of the door to see him. As he passed many years ago, that was something unusual. Then she growled at me for eating the Christmas cake and that had been eaten months beforehand. A few little things, she spent three mornings in a row calling at the back door for her dog."

I blink; the dog had been dead for at least ten years. "Did you mention it to anyone?"

"It's not my place to comment on my employers." She hunches her shoulders. "I did tell Michael that she was a little distracted when he came by. I don't believe your parents noticed anything unusual; if they did, they didn't say anything to me."

I lean back in the chair, trying to fit the pieces of the puzzle together. What if my father's affair is an illusion, perhaps triggered by Michael telling her about my problems with John? If he had no idea about her accusations, he'd lose his mind, but what if it is true and my grandmother confronted my father with the photographs from the private detective and he'd shredded them? If so, there will be nothing in the house for me to find. I consider my next plan of action. "If the evidence is gone, I need to contact the private detective and set up a meeting. I'll also go and see if I can discover any details about my grandmother's condition when she arrived at the hospital. Do you know if she'd been hurt at all?"

"I didn't see a mark on her and I'm certain your father didn't hurt her." Mrs. Jarvis looks horrified. "He'd never do such a thing. I've been with your family for thirty years and I've never seen him raise his hand to any of you. I admit when I heard them arguing he sounded extremely angry and the gist of the conversation was that she should mind her own business. When I took your grandmother her dinner, she was a little distant but she looked fine. Your father ate his pizza in the family room. He'd fallen asleep in front of the TV when I walked past to go to bed at a little after ten. I heard your mother's Lexus drive into the garage soon after. I assume your mother woke him when she came home. Apart from the argument, I don't believe your father has anything to do with the death of your grandmother. Of course the argument could have caused a stroke but I'm not a doctor so I couldn't tell you for sure. That's something you'll have to discuss with her specialist."

I nod. My forward path is clear. I need to talk to the doctor and hope he'll give me a straight answer. The thought my father might have caused Grandma's death is sending chills down my spine. I must contact the private detective and hope that he'll hand over all the information he gave to my grandmother. How I'm going to explain the cost to John, who watches every transaction on my credit card like a hawk, I have no idea. I guess I'll cross that bridge when I come to it.

FIFTEEN

NOW

I've read and reread the same paragraph in the romance novel for the last hour or so. I keep nodding off and come awake suddenly. The day has exhausted me but my mind is working well. Lying back in the pillows, I close my eyes but they snap open at the sound of giggling. I roll over and stare at the rose garden. The endless beds move slightly in the breeze and send delightful aromas through the open window. I blink as two identical girls run along the pathway and, behind them, I see the smiling face of my mother. Her arms are filled with roses. I push up, gaping at the window. I must make her hear me. "Mom, girls."

I struggle from the bed and grab my walker and then move so slowly across the floor. My mother and the girls have moved out of sight. I scream her name from the top of my voice. "Mom."

Nothing.

I'm desperate now and fling myself at the open window. "Emily, Olivia." Tears stream down my cheeks. I recall some words that alert people more than others. "Help! Fire!"

"What on earth is happening in here?" Dolly comes running into the room. "What's on fire?"

I turn to look at her. "My mother and twins are in the garden. I need to see them."

"That's impossible, I only spoke to your mother recently and told her the restrictions of your visitors at this time." Dolly grips me by the arm and leads me back to the bed.

I dig in my heels. "I saw them outside in the rose garden. Please go outside and check. Perhaps she came by with my girls to see me after all?"

"I will if you get back into bed." Dolly opens a drawer and takes out a prepared needle.

I don't have time to object as she jabs me in the thigh. Seconds later the room moves in and out of focus. I try to fight the drug but it's useless.

Darkness envelops me, thick and suffocating. It's as if a thick curtain is drawn across my mind and I can't reach out and push it back. The drug clings like a heavy fog to my thoughts blurring reality into dreams.

I open my eyes. How long have I been asleep? Darkness presses against the windows and the house is silent. I blink rapidly, struggling to piece together what had happened. Did I really hear my children's laughter and catch a glimpse of their faces or had I been dreaming? I can still see them so clearly in my mind's eye and the way their long blonde hair bounced across their shoulders. The giggles were as familiar as breathing. Were they really here?

A sound pulls me from the murky haze. The persistent ringing of a phone is coming from the direction of the office. The phone in that room doesn't work. I try to rise but my limbs are sluggish. It's as if each one is carrying a great weight. I fight with all my strength to sit up and throw my legs over the edge of the bed. By the time I grasp my walker, my breath is ragged and my body slick with sweat. I move on trembling legs, the ringing a beacon in the distance. Panic grips me, and I push my shaking legs harder. I *must* answer the phone. It's my one chance to reach the outside world. Each step is an agonizing effort but finally I stumble through the shadowed room and head for the desk. The receiver is slippery against my soaking palms. "Hello?"

The phone is dead.

Shadows close in around me, and my heart pounds as I clutch the receiver. I replace it in the cradle and stare at it, willing it to ring again but the silence is deafening. Questions race through my mind. Was it real? Was anything that happened today real? Am I living in my own alternate reality? What am I going to do? The anonymous warning echoes through my mind. *Don't trust anyone.*

I grip the edge of the desk and take a few deep breaths before moving slowly along the passageway and back to my prison. As I struggle to climb back into the bed, the first rays of sunlight break through the gloom, spreading gold across the roses, their petals sparkling with dew. The suffocating silence is broken with the early morning birdsong. It gives me hope as I struggle to stay awake and stay sane. The only one I can trust is myself.

SIXTEEN

6 MONTHS BEFORE THE ACCIDENT

I've been spending far too much time searching through the diary. It's becoming an obsession. The private detective has been evasive. He completely refused to discuss the case with me and share any findings he had given to my grandmother. I offered him a substantial retainer for the information and even showed him the letter but he made it abundantly clear that he would not help me discover the truth. I've since placed the investigation into the hands of my own private investigator but my funds are limited until the estate goes through probate. As my grandmother's concerns have been consuming my waking moments, I'm glad Michael encouraged me to join the art classes. It's been great to get out of the house and meet new people. I hadn't realized so many of the residents of our gated community are in my age bracket.

I went one day and now I go three or four times a week to work on my mess-terpiece. I admit it is a mess, although I find the process strangely compelling or perhaps it's the people and being able to talk about anything other than work and children. The man who works beside me is incredibly creative. The land-scape evolving from under his brush needs no instruction from anyone. Me? Well, I'm constantly asking the teacher if she will offer me advice on how to do this or that. It will take time but I'm getting the hang of it. The handsome man working beside me is Alex, a published author and working on his next best-seller. He claims to use his time at the art studio as his thinking time. Immersing himself into his art is a creative process that relaxes his mind.

I find him fascinating; not in a physical attraction way, but because he's so different from anyone else I've ever met. His views of the world are simplistic and not dominated by money. Living in a family of stockbrokers my entire life means conversation is about business and it's refreshing to talk about other things like his trips overseas. I've been going to lunch with him after our sessions and it's totally innocent. I laugh a lot at his antics. He listens to me and remembers everything I've told him. It's like having a second brother. My time at the art studio is giving my life meaning again. I've enjoyed myself so much I've completely forgotten it's my birthday. I arrive home and discover a red SUV parked in the driveway with a big blue bow. I climb out of my old GMC and stare at it in disbelief.

The front door is flung open and John steps out. I don't ever recall him coming home at lunchtime. I smile at him. "What are you doing home? Has the office burned down or something?"

"I wanted to be here when your birthday present arrived. I can't stay too long." John comes to my side and slips an arm around my shoulder. "Happy birthday, Jessie." He hands me a set of keys and then presses a kiss to my cheek.

I've never liked the color red and John is aware of this, so I'm a little confused about his choice but not wanting to appear ungrateful I turn and give him a bright smile. "It's wonderful, thank you."

"Where have you been all day?" John flicks a gaze over me and his nose wrinkles. "Have you been dumpster diving or something? Or do I need to increase your allowance to buy some decent clothes?"

My allowance. Yes, I know it sounds terrible for a wife to have an allowance but it's something that a husband intent on controlling every cent insists on. It's not as if we're short of money; in fact, we're considered wealthy. It's just something he has inside him. I recall when we first married, he told me to make every cent count. I had no idea at the time how controlling he would be. I nod, agreeing to his question. "Yes, an increase of my allowance would be good. There are a few things I need extra this month. I've been taking art classes. It helps pass the time when you're working and I get to speak to other people rather than sit at home alone all the time."

"You have friends at the tennis club, and it means you get plenty of exercise." John examines my face. "They're the sort of people that you need to mix with. I don't know any of the people at the art class. If you require lessons, you should be getting them from a professional not a local society."

I move the car keys from hand to hand. They're still warm from John's pocket. "John, it's just a bit of fun, a break from the monotony of life. You should try it sometime." I walk toward the vehicle and I'm suddenly nervous. It's way more powerful than my old one. I open the door and peer inside. It has that new car smell. "Everyone is driving these at the moment, they're very popular."

"I'm glad you like it." John has a satisfied look on his face. "I need to get back to the office. I'll see you tonight. Don't wait up."

SEVENTEEN

I've been driving the new car for a week now, and each time I'm out, I feel as if someone is following me. I admit I do like the features but I prefer my old car. I could park it anywhere and no one knew I was there. Being white, it blended into parking lots. This one sticks out like a sore thumb and makes it difficult for me to avoid people I don't really want to spend time with. We all have those, right? Those who gather information about you and then pass it on as if they're the community police. I could count at least five living close by who spend their time stickybeaking on other people. If one blade of grass is out of place, they'll write a letter to the community management.

Once a week my mom picks up the girls and they go out after school to spend some time with her and my dad. My mother told me that having a grandparents' day was very important and something that she always looked forward to when we were little. I've been spending more time at the art studio. Having a housekeeper coming in daily to clean and prepare meals means that there is practically nothing for me to do. I played tennis the other day and listened to the nonsensical twitter from my friends. They are so self-indulgent, being with them is more boring than watching paint dry. The paint I would prefer to watch dry is on my canvas at the studio. I climb into the SUV and head along Main, the awful feeling of someone watching me creeps over me again. It's happening more often now. I check over my shoulder, looking to see if somebody's there. Panic grips me. It's there again; the same truck is following me.

Throwing caution to the wind, I take evasive action. I brake hard and turn left, weave through traffic. I fly through a light just as it changes to red and make a right, my back wheels squealing on the blacktop. The truck is on my tail. I can't breathe. I accelerate and then brake hard again. I make a right, overtake three vehicles then turn hard left.

The truck is still there.

Frantic, I slide between two SUVs. I need to be with people and head to the art studio. My heart is pounding so fast by the time I finally arrive, I can't think straight. I park my bright-red tomato in a field of gray and white vehicles. Chills run down my spine and the truck slows and then drives past. I climb from the car and with trembling legs run into the studio. I find Alex working on his picture. Relief floods over me and I smile at the sight of him, palette in one hand, a brush clamped between his teeth as he waves another to create magic on the canvas.

"You look upset." Alex examines my face. "Everything okay?"

I want to tell him everything but he'll figure I'm crazy. "I had some guy almost run into my SUV. It shook me up some."

"Wow. Are you okay? You can relax, it's all over now." He goes back to his painting.

I wish it was but I know it's not over. I didn't imagine the truck. I shrug. "Yeah, I'll be fine as soon as I stop shaking."

We work all afternoon until the sun dips behind the trees. The natural light is slowly fading in the studio as Alex recounts one of his publishing antidotes and his laugh echoes through the room. I force a smile but my thoughts are elsewhere. I catch a flicker of movement from the corner of my eye. A shadow moves in the bushes and fear crawls up my spine. Is someone outside the window watching us? I stare into the gloom and see nothing. Perhaps it's just a bird or a trick of the light. I push the thoughts to one side and gather my brushes to clean them but the sensation that someone is out there watching me refuses to leave. I'm staring at the window seeing my own reflection. Shadows move and my heart races.

"What's so interesting out there?" Alex's voice breaks through my thoughts. "You look like you've seen a ghost." His warm curious eyes search my face.

I shake off the unease. "Oh, I was just thinking about my girls. They're having an afternoon with their grandparents. I'm glad I'm here today because it's so empty in the house without them after school. John doesn't get home until late." I meet his gaze. "He's a stockbroker and works long hours."

"Maybe he'll be able to retire early and you can go on a trip around the world." He chuckles. "Now that would make a good plot, add in a little intrigue, maybe an illicit affair or mistaken identity and have the cops chasing you." He taps his head. "I'm sorry. I can't turn it off."

I gather my things and grin at him. "I enjoy listening to your stories. I really need to buy one of your books."

"I'll bring you one." He wiggles his eyebrows. "I'm done for today and need to get home. I'll walk you to your car." Alex drops his brushes in a pot of turpentine and wipes his hands on a towel. "I need to work on my book tonight."

It's nice to have him standing there as I climb into my SUV and I give him a wave as he heads for his vehicle. My phone chimes and I look down to see my mother's name on the caller ID. "Hi Mom, is there a problem with the girls?"

"No, of course not. As there's no school tomorrow, and there's a kids' movie playing at the local theater, we wondered if you'd

allow them to stay over tonight and then you could come by and spend the day with us tomorrow. No doubt, John will have his nose to the grindstone."

I agree but the idea of walking into an empty house and spending another evening alone suddenly unnerves me. "They'll love that and I need to help you pack up Grandma's things. We should send her clothes to Goodwill."

"She asked me to go through her things and I've been working through the rooms. I know you want everything left as she had it but there's a ton of junk as well. She hoarded newspapers and so many bits of rubbish. They need to go. They're a fire hazard." She sighs. *"I still can't believe she's gone but those last few months, she changed so much. Arguing with your dad and insisting he retire came right out of the blue. I didn't want to leave her alone but I've been looking forward to moving to Florida. I'll miss you and the girls and I know you'll come for a visit but I doubt I'll come back here. For me, it's more like a prison than a home."*

I listen in disbelief. "Really, I never knew." I look around as the parking lot empties and unease slides over me. "I'm on my way home. Have a great time and I'll see you in the morning." I disconnect and start the engine. I need to get away from here.

EIGHTEEN

As I drive home, the feeling of being watched intensifies. My attention moves from the road to the rearview mirror every few seconds. Behind me, I see a row of headlights, each blinding me from the car behind them. I take a right and then another until I go around in a square, and one of the sets of lights stays with me. I catch a glimpse of the front grill as it turns the corner. Is it the same truck that followed me earlier? I can't be sure but each turn seems to bring it closer. I slow down as the lights turn orange and then gun the motor and flash through the intersection just before they turn red. I need to get away from the person following me, and I take the turn into my driveway way too fast. The garage door cranks open slowly. "Come on, come on, hurry."

I grip the steering wheel until my knuckles whiten, waiting for the gap to grow big enough for me to slide my SUV inside. I slam my hand on the door-shutting remote and sit trembling behind the wheel with the doors locked until it clicks shut. My legs shake as I rush to the door and fumble with the key to get inside the house.

This is another thing I insisted on that I regret now. Most

people can walk directly from their locked garage and into their mudroom but I insisted on having a deadbolt between the two. My palms are slick with sweat by the time I turn the doorknob and it takes one or two tries to get it to turn without slipping. I fall inside the door and stare into shadows clinging to the corners. I've never been terrified in my own home before and the sensation chills me to the bone. The alarm is buzzing and I have a few seconds to put in the code. Once the buzzing ceases, I reset the alarm and lean against the door panting.

Headlights flash across the windows. Someone is turning around—or are they? I can see the brightness through the front windows as they pause outside my home. A noise comes from the passageway and I spin around but see nothing, just an empty space stretching into darkness. I reach for the lights and sigh with relief as the house brightens before me. My heart is pounding so fast I can hardly catch my breath. Gathering all my courage, I walk through the house and check all the doors are locked. My phone buzzes, startling me, and almost slips from my hand. It's a message from Alex.

I had a great time today. I hope you're home safe now.

My fingers tremble as I type a quick reply and then I stare at the phone. I don't recall giving Alex my number. In fact, I consider it inappropriate. I hardly know the man. If John knew Alex has been texting me, he'll be angry. My mind goes to Ms. Lawson. I'm sure John has her number on speed dial and Alex is just a friend.

Before I have time to remove my shoes, a scratching noise comes from the window. I freeze and goosebumps crawl up my arms. Is someone trying to get inside? Panic grips me and I look around for a weapon. I edge my way along the wall to the fire-place and grab the poker. The metal feels heavy and cool in my trembling palm but I can't just stand here waiting for someone to hurt me. Watching me is one thing but breaking in is something else. My life might be in danger. Terrified, I lift the poker like a baseball bat and walk along the tiled passageway, hearing my own footsteps.

Fear is churning my belly but I stand beside the window and wait. The moment the window moves I'll strike. The scratching noise comes again but nothing happens. The pulse in my ears is so loud, and I'm shaking. The noise comes again. Dragging in a deep breath, I open the drapes a fraction of an inch and gasp at my reflection. I sag against the wall, steady myself and then look again. The noise is just an old overgrown rose bush close to the house scratching the windowpane.

I'm way too jumpy. What's wrong with me? I need to stop acting like an idiot and pull myself together. I return the poker and head into the kitchen to put on a pot of coffee and search the refrigerator for the meal my housekeeper has left me. I find a lasagna with a side salad. It's enough to feed all of us. As I slide a portion of the lasagna into the microwave to reheat and add a side salad to my plate, my phone buzzes again. It's a message from John.

I'm staying in town tonight. I'll see you sometime tomorrow.

I thumb a reply: *Take your time. I won't be here tomorrow.*

Don't be difficult, Jessie. You know how these dinner meetings can go on until late at night and you don't want me driving drunk, do you?

I decline to reply and carry my dinner into the family room. John won't allow us to eat meals in front of the TV but he's not here tonight, is he? This breaking of the rules feels like freedom and I sit down and put my feet on the coffee table. I chuckle at my small act of defiance. Watching TV doesn't help. After eating, I dump my plates in the dishwasher and head to my bedroom. Each sound brings back the gnawing feeling inside that insists someone is out there watching me. It's playing tricks with my mind. Most people have a particular thing they fear more than anything else—right? Although I hate to admit it, the one thing that frightens me is being watched and not knowing when someone is going to pounce on me.

I climb into bed but sleep eludes me. It's as if every creak of the house and rustle of the wind is feeding my growing paranoia. I really need to talk to someone about this, but who? John is more distant than ever and my mother would brush it off, saying I've always been scared of my own shadow and I need to grow up. I want to close my eyes and drift off, leaving this house behind in dreams, but darkness presses in on me, heavy and suffocating.

I know someone is out there watching.

Waiting.

NINETEEN

NOW

Steam swirls around me as I stand from the chair inside the shower. This morning I insisted on showering alone but I admit having the chair is the sensible thing to do. I wrap a towel tightly around myself, as the cool morning air chills my skin. Dolly has laid a fresh hospital gown on the chair beside the sink. I need to act as normal as possible and spend time in front of the mirror, using the moisturizer and brushing my hair until it shines. After pulling on the gown, I head out of the bathroom door. It is much easier now the door's been wedged open. It's not as if anyone will see me in the bathroom and, since the visit from John's lawyer, nobody has been by to see me.

I'm jumpy and didn't get much sleep. I rerun what happened the previous night, trying to get my head around it. The memory frightens me. Not knowing if it's true or I'm sleep-walking through a nightmare is disturbing. I can't risk telling Dolly I heard a phone ringing in the office and then discovered it was dead or she'll jab me with the needle. I should be able to trust her but she reports everything to the doctor. Is she really a friend or a spy? Right now I'm not sure.

I know I heard the phone ringing—or was it a dream? Dreams are so vivid of late but I've never been prone to sleep-walking in my life and the hard slog to the office had been real enough—hadn't it? The thing is, why would someone call and wait right until I picked up the phone before disconnecting—as if they're watching me? Dolly watches me all the time, doesn't she? I rub my temples, trying to make sense of everything. There's no reason Dolly would be working against me; she's here to help me recover—isn't she? I'm confused, as if I'm hovering between reality and dream state. Is this the plan? Is someone trying to make me question my sanity?

As I walk toward the bed, I stop mid-stride. My heart hammers in my chest at the sight of a vase on the nightstand, overflowing with dark-red roses, the petals still damp with the morning dew—the same roses I saw cradled in my mother's arms yesterday. Yet Dolly insisted she and the girls hadn't visited. How did the flowers end up in my room or is it part of a twisted game someone is playing? I'm questioning reality. Are the flowers really there or an illusion?

I push the walker closer. Panic grips me and sweat trickles down my back. I must keep it together and take small steps. The roses haven't moved or shimmered out of existence but I'm no longer sure of anything. Are they real or am I imagining them? My fingers tremble as I touch a petal but under my flesh the softness is too real and the color too vivid. I inhale the intoxicating fragrance. This is no vision. Is someone trying to send me a message? My mind sifts through the fragments of yesterday's confusion and the heartbreaking glimpse of my girls. It was so real and yet Dolly insisted she walked the grounds after I was asleep and found no trace of anyone.

Dizzy, I sit in a chair beside the window just as Maria pushes her cart into the bedroom with my breakfast. As she adjusts the overbed table and brings it to the chair, I smile at her. I must appear normal. I don't know who to trust anymore. "The roses are beautiful; did you pick them for me?"

"No, I found them on the kitchen table this morning when I arrived, already in the vase." Maria busies herself by placing my breakfast on the tray in front of me. "I assumed one of the gardeners brought them in for you. I told them you like fresh flowers inside your room."

I beckon her closer. "Can you find out? I'm sure I saw a woman in the garden with two children yesterday, but I'd been sleeping and it could have been a dream. Did you see anyone around the house late yesterday afternoon?"

"No, I was at the store yesterday afternoon until a little after four-thirty." Maria frowns. "I'll be sure to ask the gardeners when I speak to them about the flowers."

I nod, thankful that she is an ally and doesn't question my motives. "Thanks, but please don't mention it to Dolly. I don't want her to believe I'm imagining things."

"You have my word." Maria smiles. "I've given you an entire pot of coffee today. I understand that Dolly gave you an injection to make you sleep yesterday. I thought it might help you this morning. There's nothing worse than waking up after being drugged, is there?"

As the sound of footsteps come along the passageway, Maria hurries away with her head down as usual. I glance up from my plate as Dolly walks into the room; she is carrying a pile of clothes. "Your husband sent these over by courier. They're new but have been laundered for comfort. We estimated your size so I hope they will fit. He also included an assortment of your favorite cosmetics."

The pile of clothes in her hands are a mix of purples and pinks, which are my favorite colors. Just the sight of them makes me excited. I smile. It will be so good to get out of this hospital gown. I sigh. "Did he say when he would be dropping by again?"

"Oh, around ten and he's giving you time to adjust in between. He's following the doctor's instructions." Dolly lays the clothes and bag of cosmetics within my grasp. "He wants to do the right thing and make sure you recover completely."

I sip my coffee. "I'm sure he does."

"Your lawyer, Mr. Collins, called. He will be arriving at nine-thirty and your husband's lawyer at ten." Dolly's gaze moves over my face as if assessing me. "I will be updating the doctor this morning. Have you had any more thoughts on what happened yesterday?"

So Maria came through. I can trust her. I look at Dolly and consider her words. To give myself more time to reply, I push a forkful of eggs into my mouth and chew. This is obviously a trick question, which needs an answer to pacify her. "Since I woke, I've been having some very vivid nightmares. They're about the accident but it's just troubled thoughts, it doesn't tell me what exactly happened or even who was in the vehicle. I know I'm dreaming. I fell asleep a number of times reading my book yesterday. In the story is a scene about two little girls and I guess I was thinking about my own girls when I believed I heard them outside the window. I miss my family very much, so I assume that's what triggered it. It seemed so real at the time but now on second thought it was just wishful thinking." I meet her gaze. "I'm sorry I caused you so much trouble. It won't happen again."

"It's no trouble, Mrs. Harper; that's what I'm here for." She smiles. "Your primary care is my greatest concern. Seeing you recover is the only reward I need. The fact that you understand the difference between dreams and reality is a very positive step in your recovery. I'll be sure to tell the doctor and maybe he will allow more of your family members to visit you."

I finish my breakfast as fast as possible and dive into the pile of clothes. I feel like a teenager again as I slide the designer labels over my new slim body. The fit is almost perfect, and

John has got the selection of cosmetics just right. I look young and fresh, almost the same as when we first met. At last I'll be able to hold my own in front of Ms. Lawson. I spray a little Chanel No. 5 behind each ear and smile at my reflection. Isn't it amazing how a few clothes and a little makeup can boost your ego to such an extent?

TWENTY

5 MONTHS BEFORE THE ACCIDENT

I pace the length of the kitchen, my mind racing. The private detective's report lays open on the table. I've read each word three or four times and understand what had upset my grandma so badly. I run my fingertips across the picture of a young woman and her daughter. The mother of the child looks younger than me. I can hardly breathe with the implications. The report says that my father has been providing for them in secret and visits them often. I stare at the documents and a sob catches in my throat. Has my father had an affair with a woman younger than his own daughter? Is this what upset my grandmother so much it caused her stroke? Is this the dirty little secret she wanted me to expose? God help me, these secrets killed her.

My head is spinning with indecision. I want to drive to my father's office and confront him face-to-face but fear if I get behind the wheel in this state, I will cause an accident. Is my mother aware of his deception? I need to confront him about this now. I grab my phone and call my father's number. My hands are trembling as I wait but the call goes straight to voicemail. "Why won't you ever answer your phone?"

Anger trembles through me. I need answers and I need

them now. I almost shout down the phone after the beep. "Dad, I need you to call me back. It's urgent." I disconnect and toss the phone on the table on the pile of photographs I'll never forget.

The image of my mother flashes across my mind and I moan in misery. How could he do something like this? That child could be my sister. How could he keep something so important from me—from all of us? He's denied a child her family. Suddenly the thought of confronting him makes my stomach ache but I can't let this go. I need to confide in someone. I need a second opinion to make sure I'm thinking straight and not going at this like a bull at a gate. Can I confide in Alex? He doesn't have anything to gain or lose by speaking to me and he's a good friend.

I grab my keys and drive to the little café where Alex likes to write. I find him in his usual seat in the window. He's bent over his laptop with a steaming cup of coffee in front of him. I order a hot beverage at the counter and head in his direction. As I approach, he glances up from his laptop and a wide smile stretches his lips. I try to smile back. "Hi Alex, have you got a moment for a chat?"

"Is something wrong?" His soft eyes scan my face and he frowns. "Have you eaten today?"

I sit down and push both hands through my hair. "I honestly can't remember. I guess I shouldn't come to you, but I didn't know where else to go."

"You can always talk to me, Jessie." He stares at me. "What's up?"

I swallow hard and then dive in. "It's my father. He's been providing for a woman younger than me and she has a child. I'm not exactly sure what I should do. My first instinct was to call him and demand he tell me what's going on, but my call went to voicemail, which is probably the best thing that could have happened because I don't think I'm in any fit state to be talking to him about this right now."

"That's a lot to process." Alex glances up as the server delivers my coffee. As the server walks away, he turns his attention back to me. "Do you figure the child is his?"

I have mixed emotions about the possibility—joy, because I have a new sibling, and betrayal, because I can't believe my father would lie to me. I can't put my emotions into words right now so I just shrug. "I'm not sure, but my grandma left me a letter with her lawyer, asking me to look into the secrets surrounding our family. I know she confronted my father about something the night before she suffered a stroke and never recovered."

"Oh, that's not good." Alex squeezes my hand. "I'm glad you came to me. This would be a very delicate thing to discuss with the family without knowing the full facts. At least I have an unbiased view. How did you come to discover this information?"

I tell him about my grandmother's letter and speaking to her private detective. "He wouldn't break client confidentiality even though I showed him the letter, so I engaged one myself and the documents arrived this morning. I've been reading and rereading them since they arrived, not knowing what to do." I took a long sip of the scalding coffee. "I kind of lost it and I left a message for my father to call me back. Now I don't know what I'm going to say. This bombshell could destroy our family and I don't want to be responsible for doing that."

"This isn't something you can do over the phone, Jessie, nor in front of spectators. You need to speak to him alone. There may be a perfectly reasonable explanation why he's helping this family." Alex met my gaze. "Think through what you've told me. He's your father and I assume he's been a good father to you? If so, you owe him the benefit of the doubt."

I mull over his words and nod slowly. I just knew that Alex would give me a clear and concise path to travel. "Okay, I'll go and see him. He's still working a few days a week. When he retired, both John and Michael wanted him to work at the same firm. Everyone around me are stockbrokers."

"Oh, my God, it's all making sense now." Alex slams a palm to his forehead. "Are you related to Michael Thompson?"

I narrow my gaze. "Yes, he's my brother. Why?"

"Michael is my stockbroker." Alex shook his head in disbelief. "He asked me about the art classes and mentioned it would be perfect for his sister." His brow furrows. "He said you were having problems. Is this what he was referring to?"

I shake my head and, suddenly famished, reach for a sandwich. "No, not this. It's something else. My husband works long hours and Michael suggested the art classes. I needed to meet people and chat before I lose the ability to hold a decent conversation." I take a bite of the sandwich and chew slowly. "I should go and speak to my dad this afternoon, while he's in his office. I don't want to involve my mom at this stage."

"Do you want me to come with you? I can wait outside." Alex smiles at the server as she refills the cups. "I'm very good at moral support and you might need someone to drive you home."

I smile at him. "That sounds like a plan."

"Just be careful, you might end up in one of my stories." His laugh is infectious. "The weird things that happen in Grande Haven, I can't make up."

Laughing, I turn to him. "You can say that again." I take a deep breath. "I'm glad we met. You're really a good friend, Alex, and I appreciate it." *And right now, he's the only person I trust.*

TWENTY-ONE

Having Alex behind me as I drive to my father's office has erased the horrible feeling that someone is following me. This time when I look in my rearview mirror, all I see is Alex's Ford Explorer. It is good to have him beside me as we head out of the elevator. The door swishes open and I walk straight into Michael, who gives me the strangest expression as his gaze drifts toward Alex. "I've come to see Dad." I indicate toward Alex. "Small world, isn't it? Alex is one of my art class buddies."

"Did you come to see me, Alex? I don't recall having an appointment with you today." Michael's forehead creases into a frown.

"Nope, I'm the support team." Alex smiles.

"What's going on, Jessie?" Michael flicks a glance at me. "I'm not sure if it's a good time to drop by. John is entertaining some of his clients in the conference room."

I look at him and raise an eyebrow. "You mean he's in there entertaining Ms. Lawson?" I throw both hands in the air and let them drop to my sides. "What's new?" I move past him. "Don't worry, I won't make a scene. I didn't come to see John. I came to see Dad." I look over my shoulder at Alex. "Wish me luck."

"I'll wait here." Alex drops onto the visitors' sofa. "I'm here if you need me." He chuckles. "Oh, Michael, don't look so scandalized. I'm here for moral support is all. That's what friends do for each other, don't you know?"

As I walk toward my father's office door, clutching the detective's report, my mind races with questions. I need answers and I'm not leaving without them. I pause, hand raised to knock on the door. Will this be the end of my relationship with my father? I bite down hard on my bottom lip and knock before pushing the door open. "Sorry to disturb you, Dad, but we need to talk."

"Jessie, what's wrong?" He rises from behind the desk, his face a mask of concern. "Has something happened to your mother?"

I shake my head, barely able to contain the emotions welling up inside me. "Mom's fine. This is the problem."

I toss the envelope on the desk, and my pulse thunders in my ears. "Read it."

My stomach flip-flops as he lifts the flap and pours out the contents. I watch his face as he scans the pages and his expression shifts from confusion to anger.

"Where did you get this?" He lifts his gaze to me.

I'm trembling and suddenly I'm four again, and in trouble. I suck in a deep breath to steady my nerves. I can't back down now. "Where I got it isn't important. What I need is the truth. Are you the father of that child?"

"No, I'm not." Color creeps up his neck and into his cheeks. He gathers up the report and stuffs it back in the envelope. "How could you believe such a thing?"

I meet his gaze, shaking my head. "Because you're supporting them. If that kid isn't yours then why all the secrecy? It's obvious you visit them often. Does Mom know about them?"

"We need to keep your mother out of this. It's complicated, Jessie." He leans both hands on the table and stares at me. "I can't expect you to understand and I don't need to explain myself. This is none of your business."

Tears sting the backs of my eyes. "Is that all you've got to say? Grandma found out, didn't she? You had a huge argument with her. I know that was the night she had the stroke." I dug my finger into the envelope on the table. "She died because of this."

"Don't you dare bring your grandmother into this." He leans forward on the desk. "I had nothing to do with her suffering a stroke. How could you say such a thing?"

Shaken, I take a step back. "Because she told me on her deathbed, something was going on with you. After you had that argument with her, she wrote a letter and had Maria deliver it to Mr. Collins. He gave it to me after the reading of the will. It was a warning about the secrets in the family. She wanted me to know about the secret family you're supporting."

"I don't believe you." His eyes widen in shock. "Where is this so-called letter?"

I pull the neatly folded letter from my pocket and hand it to him. "This is why she fired you, isn't it? She didn't trust you any longer. What else are you hiding? It's obvious she didn't get the full story before she died."

I stare at him as he reads the letter and notice a slight tremor in his hands. When he finally looks up at me, his eyes are filled with a mixture of anger and pain. I slam my fist down on the table. "Do you have an excuse? I'd like to hear it before I tell Mom."

"I can assure you the child is not mine." Dad shakes his head. "You have my word."

I can't believe my ears. "Your word? Then who are they?" I wait a few seconds before glaring at him. "Do you need more time to make up another lie?"

"I'm not lying." He straightens, meeting my gaze. "I'm only trying to protect you."

I shake my head in disbelief. "From what—the truth?"

"From things you don't understand, things that will destroy our family." He walks out from behind his desk and stares out of the wide window overlooking skyscrapers.

His words are like a slap in the face. "What do you mean by 'destroy our family'? Keeping secrets like this is what will tear us apart."

"The child isn't mine and that's all you need to know. I'm not discussing this with you, not now, not ever. You'll just have to trust me on this." He turns and the afternoon sunlight hits him from behind like a halo. "Some things are better left buried."

Tears stream down my cheeks. I want to trust him but everything feels like a lie, plus I made a promise to Grandma on her deathbed. "I want to believe you but right now you're not giving me any reason to."

"It was none of your grandmother's business and she as sure as hell shouldn't have involved you." He dashes a hand through his hair. "Jessie, if you care for our family, walk away now and forget this ever happened." He shakes his head, turns his back on me and walks out of the room.

I stare after him, unable to believe he just left me here. A mixture of anger, betrayal, and sorrow consumes me.

What was so terrible that it killed my grandmother, and why couldn't he trust me with the truth?

TWENTY-TWO

My mind is a whirlpool of emotions as I leave my father's office. It's as if the weight of his denial and evasiveness is pressing down on me. I desperately want to speak to John. I need his comfort and level-headedness but Michael's strained expression when he saw me arrive spoke volumes. I guess mentioning about John's meeting with Ms. Lawson was to soften the blow if I see them together. I bite back a laugh. I need comfort and someone to talk to but the person I want most is the one I can't trust. As I head for the foyer, as if on cue, I see John and Ms. Lawson emerging from the conference room. They walk, heads tipped together, their body language too close for comfort. They are so involved with each other they don't notice me. I keep walking and head for the wide glass doors.

"Jessie, are you okay?" Alex is at my side. His eyes fill with concern.

I stop walking and turn to look at him. "I'm not sure." My bottom lip is trembling and I wrap both arms around my stomach. "My dad told me to mind my own business. I've never seen him so angry and then I come out and see my husband with *her*." I indicate behind him at the couple walking toward us.

"Oh, I see." Alex shuffles his feet. "You never mentioned you had problems with your husband."

I snort with the absurdity of the situation. "I don't. I have problems with *her*."

At that moment, John's eyes meet mine and his expression shifts. Is it guilt or just surprise? In a flash, he composes himself and walks toward us with Ms. Lawson a step behind.

"Jessie, what are you doing here?" John glances at his watch. "If you'd told me you were coming, I would have made time in my schedule."

I shake my head slowly. "Some things you can't plan for, John."

"What exactly do you mean by that?" He checks his watch again. "I have a call from Hong Kong in a matter of minutes. What's wrong?"

Ms. Lawson's eyes flick to John and then back at me. She raises one perfectly arched eyebrow but says nothing. The tension in the air is thick enough to cut with a knife. I can feel Alex behind me and I meet John's curious gaze as it flicks over him. "Our house is on fire and our children are gone."

"What on earth are you talking about?" John narrows his eyebrows. "Is that some kind of sick joke?"

I laugh. "Well, I guess if it were true, I wouldn't need an appointment to see my own husband—or would I?"

"I really don't have time for this." John comes to my side and grips my arm to pull me into an alcove. "I don't appreciate you making a scene in front of my staff. If you have something to say, say it." He glances over one shoulder and then turns his attention back to me. "Who's he?"

I glare at him. "He's the moral support I need when you're too busy." I swallow hard, fighting back tears. "Never mind. I'll work it out like I always do." I drag my arm away from him. "You'd better go, you wouldn't want to be late for your dinner with Ms. Lawson."

Before he has time to reply, I toss my hair over one shoulder and head for the door. Alex follows close behind me. In the elevator, I turn to him. "I'm sorry. I didn't mean to drag you into my problems. I had no idea I'd see John with her again. The last time I ran into them it was in the new bistro. They walked right past me as if I wasn't there."

"Ouch!" Alex squeezes my arm. "I'm so sorry. Did you get things figured out with your dad?"

I shake my head. "Nope. He's so angry with me. It was terrible and now I'm more confused than ever."

"Maybe you should talk to Michael?" Alex follows me from the elevator and we take the stairs to the underground parking lot.

I stop, aware of the exhaust fumes in the enclosed area, and shrug. "Maybe, but I'm not sure if bringing him into the situation is the right thing to do. I sure as hell can't tell my mom. The information would destroy her."

"Oh, jeez. Maybe you should go and see the woman in the photographs?" Alex pushes both hands into the front pockets of his jeans and leans against a brick wall, eyebrows raised. "I'll go with you, if you want me to. Just as moral support. I don't need to know the details. You can't be expected to cope alone with lies and deceit, especially when you need an appointment to see your husband. Heavens above. I can't believe he said that to you."

He's right, of course. Going straight to the source is aways the best way of discovering information. Right now I'm confused and hurt. Both the most important men in my life have turned against me. I'm empty, drained of hope. I must at least try and turn things around. "I don't either. I'll get more information and then go and see the woman. I owe it to my grandma to discover the truth—whatever the cost."

TWENTY-THREE
NOW

Time is moving fast and excitement builds as I wait in the office for the arrival of Mr. Collins. Just speaking to someone from the outside world gives me hope of finally going home and discovering the truth about my girls. As the family lawyer, Mr. Collins has been my go-to person for legal advice for ever. I refuse to change him, even with John's insistence. He is the one person I know I can trust. I hear his lumbering footsteps coming along the passageway and push my hair behind my ears. He enters the room with an air of practiced authority; his gaze moves over me, sharp and assessing. I see him nod as if I have passed his scrutiny. "It's good to see you again, Mr. Collins. Thank you so much for coming to see me at short notice."

"Good morning, Jessie. It's good to see you up and about." Although his tone is detached, his face holds an expression of compassion. "Now what's all this about John wanting you to give him power of attorney over your portfolio and the running of the estate?"

My pulse races. "This is why I called you. I feel as if Ms. Lawson is pressuring me into making a decision I'm not convinced is right. I'm sure it's not something my grandma wanted me to do. She was very specific that John was to have nothing to do with the running of the business. You know that, don't you? Before Grandma died, I became suspicious that John is having an affair with his lawyer and told Michael in confidence and he told Grandma. I've no proof, but I'm concerned because John spends all his time with her."

"As she is the corporate lawyer of his firm, it would be normal for him to spend time with her." Mr. Collins peers at me over the top of the glasses balancing halfway down his nose. "I know his occupation is extremely time-consuming and lunch meetings are quite normal in that profession. Many stockbrokers hold dinner parties for prospective clients. As we're talking about millions of dollars, no expense is spared. If this is what you're seeing, it would be easy for you to assume John is having an affair. Have you spoken to him about it? I'm sure after all this time he would have divorced you by now, if there was any interest in another woman. He is wealthy in his own right and the prenup you signed means he can literally walk away. As this hasn't happened, I believe you should give him the benefit of the doubt until you know for sure one way or the other."

I shake my head slowly. "Let's take John out of the equation for just a moment. This is about respecting my grandmother's last wishes. You will recall I was at her bedside when she died?" I fold my arms across my chest. "She was so torn up about what she discovered about my father; when Michael told her about John's alleged affair, she freaked out. I believe toward the end she didn't trust anyone."

"Is this something you need to discuss with me, Jessie?" Mr. Collins' concerned gaze meets mine. "Everything we speak about is confidential."

I tell him everything I remember. "I did have photographs and a report from a private detective but I hid them somewhere and I can't recall where. They're probably at my house."

"How did this all come about?" Mr. Collins' eyebrows raise.

I run memories through my mind. "I'm still a little vague on the details but after you gave me Grandma's letter, I recall searching for documents before the accident and finding nothing apart from a diary which seems to have mysteriously vanished. I confronted my father and he told me to mind my own business." I sigh. "So now you know the reason why Grandma changed her will, what are my options?"

"Jessie, considering that you've just come out of a coma, and your memory of that time hasn't returned, we have to consider your ability to manage the estate. As executor of your grand-mother's will, it's my duty to ensure the estate is handled prop-erly. At the moment, the portfolio is being handled by Legacy Securities, a firm engaged by your grandmother prior to her death. I can see no reason to remove the portfolio from that company and transfer it to John, especially knowing the circum-stances. Although, I'm sure his firm would be more than happy to take on such a lucrative property."

I look at him, not completely understanding. "My grand-mother left me the property in her will... surely now that I'm awake I can take control of it?"

"This is where we come to a legal problem." Mr. Collins blinks a few times as if trying to get his words into order. "This is one of the reasons you've been kept isolated from everyone including social media and television. The will categorically states that you must be of sound mind to inherit. So I'm over-seeing the estate and making all the decisions necessary to give you as much time as possible to recover. I don't have a time limit on this as probate takes as long as it takes. Until I am satisfied one way or the other, nothing is being transferred to anyone." He sighs. "It was your grandmother's wishes that you inherit her estate and I will do everything in my power to ensure that happens."

My mind spins. This can't be happening. I'm not of sound

mind just because I can't remember the couple of days before the accident? That could be a medical condition I have no control over. "Not recalling the accident doesn't make me not of sound mind, does it? I am in control of my faculties. I'm not brain damaged. Many people can't recall alarming things that happened to them. It's when the brain protects us from bad memories. The thing is, I remember the accident but what I can't recall is the day it happened."

"It's not how I feel about you personally." Mr. Collins removes his glasses to clean them, all the time eyeing me with interest. "I would get a doctor's assessment if I needed one but our problem is those people who want your inheritance. They will try and make a court believe they have proof you're unbalanced."

I swallow the bile in my mouth. "Unbalanced? What makes me appear that way? Is it because I've demanded to know if my kids are alive and well?" I look at him and see the truth. "That's why they sedated me, isn't it, to make me look crazy? And every time they drugged me they made notes. Can they use that against me?"

"Unfortunately they can try." Mr. Collins peered at me over the top of his spectacles.

I stare at Mr. Collins, not knowing how to respond, but suddenly the crazy things happening around me make sense. Seeing my kids in the garden, the phone call late at night, and the roses this morning. Are they all part of some sinister plot to unhinge me? If so, who would benefit? Only I know what's written in the will, well, apart from Mr. Collins and he wouldn't tell anyone. Michael would benefit but he's overseas and living in blissful ignorance of the terms of the will. I clear my throat. "So if I sign the document to give John power of attorney, as nothing is mentioned in the will to prevent him, he could in fact, take control of my inheritance. Is that correct?"

"Yes, indeed he can. He is married to you and you have every legal right to give him power of attorney if you feel that you're incapable of running the estate. Once you put that in writing I'll have no option but to transfer the estate. He'll be acting on your behalf."

I nod as the implications sink deep, churning my gut. "Can I revoke it when I'm well?"

"Yes, it would be easy in normal circumstances but if John protests your decision, you may need to prove in court that you're of sound mind." Collins sighs. "It could become messy. If you want my professional advice, I would give yourself at least a month or so to get your head on straight. I don't believe after less than a week you should be making decisions like this, when the estate is not in any danger. Everything is going along exactly as it did when your grandmother was in charge. If anything changes, I will inform you."

A knock comes on the door and Maria steps inside. "Mr. Harper and Ms. Lawson are here. Do you want me to show them in?"

I nod. "Yes, of course, we've been waiting for them."

Ms. Lawson walks into the room in a cloud of fragrance, dressed as if she'd just stepped off the front page of *Vogue*. She gives me a tight smile and waits for John to pull out a chair for her, as if it's a natural thing for him to do. As she reaches into her briefcase, I notice she isn't wearing my bracelet this time. I shoot a glance at John, my suspicions flaring anew, because in its place is a sparkling new diamond bracelet. She places the documents on the table and then acknowledges Mr. Collins. I lean forward, my gaze moving to my lawyer. "Mr. Collins, may I introduce you to Ms. Lawson?"

"Let's cut straight to the chase." Ms. Lawson ignores me completely and directs her conversation toward my lawyer. "This is a very simple power of attorney issue, to ensure your client's property is handled in the family. The estate has been in limbo for over twelve months. It's time to move on. I'm sure you would appreciate having this responsibility removed from your desk."

I ignore her completely and look straight at John. "After speaking with Mr. Collins, I've decided not to sign. You're assuming that I'm not capable of running the estate. I agree, I haven't remembered everything before the wreck, but things are coming back really fast, and I'd prefer to leave everything status quo for a few more weeks until I can get on my feet again. I'm sure you understand?"

"Mr. Collins, please speak to your client about the necessity of doing this?" Ms. Lawson's eyes flash with anger.

"This is all we've been speaking about since I arrived." Mr. Collins opens his hands. "I gave my advice and I'm taking my client's directions."

"Can we have a moment alone, Jessie?" John steps away from the door and looks at me before turning his attention to the lawyers. "It will only take a minute."

As Collins and Ms. Lawson leave the room, John sits on the corner of the desk. He slides close to me and reaches inside his pocket. He produces a velvet pouch and pours my bracelet and wedding ring onto his palm. He takes my hand and gently kisses my knuckles before slipping my wedding ring on my finger. The fit is loose. It seems I've lost weight on my fingers as well. I clasp my hand into a fist and stare into his mesmerizing blue eyes. He takes my other hand and attaches the bracelet; it was always a little tight but now is a perfect fit. My stomach gives that little flutter that always happens when he's close, but does he belong to me or is this a ruse to make me sign the documents?

I stare at the jewelry. I should be overjoyed but my mind is a whirlpool of confusion and suspicion. I grip my hands together to stop them trembling and it soon passes. The weight of the bracelet is strangely comforting as if it's come home. I want to believe so much that John cares, I ache for him but is this an olive branch or another manipulation? I can see by his expression he is waiting for a reaction, for me to say how wonderful it is he's returned my jewelry. "Why are you giving these back to me now? You could have brought them when I regained ·consciousness. Do you know how horrible it was to wake up and find my wedding ring missing? It was like being abandoned. You know I've never removed my wedding ring or that bracelet since the day we married. As they mean so much to me, I expected you to give them back to me right away."

"I didn't expect you to live, Jessie." He heaves a sigh. "I've carried them in my pocket since they took you to the hospital." John's gaze is steady but distant. "Right now, I need you to trust me." His lips raise in a half-smile. "You know I'm the best man for the job of running the portfolio. Collins is barely paying for the upkeep of the house. Sign the papers, Jessie. It's in our best interests."

Trust him? How can I when he won't even tell me about my girls? His hand cups my cheek and he bends to kiss me. It's so soft and intimate I want to lean into him and lose myself. Is he using his charm to manipulate me? Nothing is making sense anymore. I don't know my friends, and weird things keep happening. Time seems to blend together in a maddening deception. I'm suffocating and the walls are closing in around me. Gasping for breath, I push away from him. "I don't know what's real anymore."

"Then let me help you. Sign the papers, Jessie, and I'll take care of everything." John's hand drops from my cheek and his expression hardens. "You know it's the right thing to do."

He acts so loving and, yet, is it a ploy to get my entire inheritance? It could never happen but he doesn't know that, does he? He believes the wills we made together leaving everything to the survivor are still current but I changed mine, leaving the Stonebridge estate in its entirety to Michael.

I look at John, willing my mind to accept his word but what if he orchestrated everything that's happened since I regained consciousness to make me look as if I'm losing my mind? It would mean I'm not competent to inherit the estate. I'm falling into a whirlpool of indecision. How can I possibly trust him when nothing makes sense. How can I trust anyone?

TWENTY-FOUR

4 MONTHS BEFORE THE ACCIDENT

The last couple of weeks have been brutal. John believes I'm losing my mind. He considers my concerns about my father ridiculous and a manifestation of an overactive imagination. He just can't understand why I need to spend time with him. His main focus is on his work, and his ambition to rise to the top of his profession is more important than anything. He'll allow nothing to stand in his way—including me. He spends more and more time away from home now and last week I moved my things into the spare room. I just can't stand feeling the empty space beside me in bed night after night. The last time he came home he didn't even seem to notice I wasn't there. We've missed a few of the local celebrations, and people are starting to talk, so I avoid the tennis club and the nosy so-called friends, who spy into every detail of my marriage. The only place I find respite is at the art studio. I've slowly been replacing the pictures the decorator placed on our walls with some of my own. Each of them holds a special memory, a tiny glimpse into a time when I was laughing and without a worry in the world.

Alex is a good friend and someone who wants nothing more from me than a smile. I've read a few of his books and find them fascinating, much like the man himself. My private investigator has given me all the details I require to visit Andrea Long. I know everything about her now. She is much younger than I imagined and the poor woman must have had her daughter very young. This knowledge frightens me. Why is my father involved with her? Was she underage when she had her child? The entire scenario makes me hesitant to look deeper into the situation. If the child isn't my father's as he professes, then who is the father? I take out my grandmother's letter and read it again. I scan the pages of her diary, searching for clues. Why would my father hide this secret if he wasn't involved? I don't have any uncles or any other close family members apart from Michael.

I rub my hands over my face. I've seen Michael's girlfriends. Even at college, he set his sights on older women. I recall my father lecturing him in the study, when he insisted on dating a divorcee. I couldn't imagine him being involved with an underage girl. I pick up the documents the private investigator sent me and I check the date of birth of the child. She was born the year after I married John. I press my fist into my mouth to stop myself screaming. No wonder my father has kept this information from everyone. He was protecting me from the terrible truth. There is only one logical conclusion—the child belongs to John.

I can't keep this to myself any longer. I call Michael and insist he comes by right away. I pace up and down the family room, waiting for him to arrive. On the kitchen table I've laid out all the damning information. Will he come to the same conclusion as I have? When he arrives, we sit at the table with steaming cups of coffee before us. The subject is so delicate I've been considering exactly what to say but when the time comes it's difficult to get the words out. "You know what John's been like since we married? At first, I believed he still considered himself to be single. The way he acted toward me wasn't like a husband proud of his new wife. I was more like a friend that he could leave in the corner when he got bored with me. I talked to Mom about it and she said that young men all go through a period of adjustment. Until recently, I believed that was the case, but after seeing John with Ms. Lawson, I realize he's never been that attentive to me. It's as if I've become a habit, or the person he married to make himself look good. My family name could enhance his career. Now he has everything he wants, I've become redundant."

"I've never heard him say a bad word about you, Jessie." Michael leans back in his chair, regarding me closely. "Although, I won't lie to you, I do admit he's very attentive to Ms. Lawson. I would say they are very close friends. I don't believe it would be in your best interest to come between them."

My gut clenches as if he's spoken all my fears. "Yes, well, I tried that and now he very rarely comes home. Do you know where he stays?"

"I believe he stays in his apartment in Manhattan." Michael turns his coffee cup around with the tips of his fingers. "You knew about that, right?"

I shake my head, and my stomach slips to my boots. "No, I didn't know. He doesn't tell me anything." I wave my hand toward the pile of documents on the table. "As you know, I was at Grandma's bedside when she died. She couldn't speak but we communicated and she intimated Dad had a secret that involved me. Over these last few months I've been trying to discover what's going on. Grandma left me a letter with Mr. Collins, written the day she died. It involves a young woman and child that Dad has been providing for. It's been going on for about seven years."

"What are you talking about?" Michael's eyebrows rise to his hairline.

I hold up a hand to hush him. "The day I dropped by your office with Alex, I confronted Dad about the woman and child.

He went ballistic and told me to mind my own business. The thing is, Michael, I'm starting to believe that Dad has been covering up for John and that's what Grandma discovered."

"You've gone too far this time, Jessie." Michael picks up the documents and tosses them into the trash. "Dad's right, whatever this is about it's none of your business." He sighs. "This obsession with Grandma's letter and Dad's secrets is consuming you. You're never home. You spend all your time at the art studio with Alex. Think about it? Is this the reason John isn't coming home?"

Shocked by his reaction, I stare at him in disbelief. I'm at home all the time the girls are out of school and his comment stings. Angry, I slam a hand on the table. "You figure this is *my* fault? I'm not the one that's been keeping secrets for years. Look at the documents, they prove Grandma was right."

"Do they? Look, Jessie, you've been through a lot lately and I know how close you were to Grandma. Stress can cloud your judgment." Michael rubs the back of his neck. "Think about it: you're gathering scraps of information and jumping to conclusions. How do you figure this looks? How do you believe the family will react? Everyone's worried about you, Jessie. Since Grandma died you haven't been the same."

I grip my coffee cup as doubt creeps in. "I trusted you and you're trying to make me look crazy."

"Oh Jessie, I'm just trying to help you." Michael comes around my side of the table and puts an arm around my shoulders. "Being with Grandma when she died was very traumatic. Speak to John and tell him what's happened. If not, I have a great therapist you can see if you decide to speak to someone."

I grip my cup so tight my fingers turn white. "No. I can't let this go. I made Grandma a promise. It's pointless talking to John. If he's involved, he's hardly going to admit it, is he? He knows if it gets out, it will ruin him. That's not my intention. I just want the truth. As his wife, he owes me that." I turn to look at him. "You need to pick a side. Either you're with me or against me."

"Okay, but promise me you'll be careful." Michael blows out a long sigh. "Digging up the past can lead to more pain than answers."

TWENTY-FIVE

NOW

I need to get away. John's presence is overpowering, his magnetism drawing me toward him, taking away my will. After all I've been through with him, nothing diminishes the love I have for him. It's like a chain around my neck holding me back from making decisions. I've always believed that love is something a person should cherish and not use against others. My mind flashes back to a chat I had with an old friend from school. Jane was a straight shooter and I miss her terribly since she was lost at sea in a boating accident. I confided in no one but her about my suspicions early on in my marriage. She told me to take the girls and leave, that John wasn't worth it and I could get anyone I wanted. I told her I could never leave him and she said I remind her of an old faithful dog that the owner chains up, when they don't have time for it. Her words flow into my mind and I stagger to my feet.

I feel vulnerable using the walker; being weak will give John another excuse not to be with me heart and soul. One thing is for sure, he'll never let his clients see me like this. I wonder sometimes why he chose me, as it's obvious by the way he parades Ms. Lawson that he really wanted a trophy wife.

Another memory breaks into my consciousness, a smiling face and an infectious laugh. I need to concentrate to bring the fuzzy image to life. It comes back in a rush. I remember everything. *Alex.*

I grip the handles of the walker and move painfully slowly to the door. The memory of my friend Alex lightens my mood. I wonder if he knows I'm awake or even alive? Heat rushes up my neck and into my cheeks as I turn to John. "I'm going to the library. I need a little time to think."

"I'm so proud of you, Jessie." John opens the door and stands to one side. "It's only been a week and look at you getting around. Dolly has been giving you physical therapy to keep your muscles strong but I'll ask her to recommend a physical therapist. I'll make sure they come by as often as necessary to help you increase your strength, then you won't need to rely on the walker."

I turn to look at him and see compassion in his eyes. Am I seeing the truth or is this another illusion? "That would be good, thank you. I would really like a phone and a line of credit so I can purchase the things I need."

"Just ask Dolly what you need and she'll get it for you." John frowns. "Who do you need to contact?"

I shake my head and look at him. "I needed to speak to Mr. Collins and I figured maybe you might want to talk to me from time to time. It's very lonely here. I know Dolly looks after me really well and I'm sure she's trying to be a friend but I've been restricted from having visitors. I can't see my family and yet you allowed two women I hardly know to visit the other day."

"I did no such thing. I wasn't informed of any visitors." John frowns and the wrinkles in his forehead mar his perfect features. "I didn't want my mother to come here either but she had a bee in her bonnet and had made arrangements before you woke. You know what she's like, always trying to organize everybody." He sighs. "You say you didn't recognize the visitors?"

I snort a laugh. "Is this a trick question?"

"No, of course it isn't, why would you think such a thing?" John looks abashed.

I push my walker toward the library. "Don't worry about it. Why don't you take Ms. Lawson down to the kitchen? Maria will make her a cup of coffee or whatever fancy tea she drinks. I'm sure you'll need a few moments to chat to Mr. Collins." I turn and shoot him a long look. "Don't worry, I'm not going anywhere."

I bypass the library as John enters the family room and ushers Mr. Collins and Ms. Lawson back into the office, no doubt to discuss my state of mind. I'm on the ground floor and gather it's the only floor not closed and with the furniture draped in dust covers. Many years ago, the ground floor was for the servants. Now many of the staff live in the cottages spread across the expanse of the estate. I make my way to the kitchen and find it empty. My heart pounds as I glide across the floor to the telephone. It's a landline attached to the wall and has been there since I was a child. Beside it on a small table is a notepad and a jar of pens resting on top. My heart picks up the pace as I lift the receiver. I press the number for directory assistance and excitement rushes through me at the sound of a voice. I give Alex's name and address. The voice gives me a number and I hurry to write it down. I press in the number, so slowly, terrified of making a mistake. I look all around and listen for footsteps. A familiar voice answers the phone. "Alex? It's Jessie. I'm alive."

"Jessie? Oh my goodness, it's so good to hear your voice. Where are you?"

I tell him and give him a brief explanation of why I'm calling. "I sneaked down to the kitchen to use the phone. They've cut me off from everyone, well, apart from my lawyer, and I insisted that he come. They want me to sign everything over to John. I believe they're trying to make out I'm losing my mind."

"I've heard nothing about you from anyone since the accident." He sounds calm and his usual self. *"There was a small column in the local newspaper saying that you were in a coma. Another said you were brain-dead and your husband was going to make the heartbreaking decision to turn off your life support. I honestly believed you died, even though I didn't see any funeral notices in the paper. I asked after you, but Michael refused to talk about the accident, saying it was just too disturbing."*

I listen with interest. "So you knew about the accident? Do you know what happened? I can't recall a thing, about that night or maybe a few days prior. My life was in a mess. I can remember everything that happened with my father. Over the last twenty-four hours or so everything is coming back to me about that time. I recall going to the office with you to speak to my father and the fallout. After that it becomes a little fuzzy but it's only been a week." I take a deep breath. "Can you come and see me and help me sort out my mind? I need to know what happened that night."

"Everything I know about that night is hearsay. You know Grande Haven lives on gossip." He clears his throat. *"Are you sure you want to know about this?"*

Sweat trickles down my back as I scan all around, waiting to be caught. "Yes, I do, but I haven't got much time. They've disabled all the phones in the house apart from this one. I have no communication with anyone. Their excuse is that I need to discover the truth myself."

"If that's what the doctors believe is best for you, maybe I shouldn't get involved?"

I feel my only chance slipping away. "Please, Alex, you're the only person I can trust."

"Okay I'll try but they might not let me in." I could hear him walking from one room to the other. *"I'll come and see you tomorrow. In the meantime I'll hunt around and see if I can find*

out any other information for you. The only thing I know for sure is that you had an argument with John, that went on for some time before you left in the SUV. It was around ten and they didn't find you until after midnight."

I hear doors opening along the passageway and panic grips my stomach. "I'll see you tomorrow. You'll need the code to get through the gate, so write it down. There's a keypad on the driver's side." I give him the details. "Don't use the front door. Walk around the house until you find a rose garden. There's a conservatory at the back of the house with a door to the garden. The conservatory leads to a passageway and to a sunroom and that's where I am." A noise in the passageway makes my heart race. "Someone is coming and they can't know that I've used the phone. I must go."

"I'll find you."

Voices echo along the empty passageway, as I hang up the receiver. I shuffle to the counter, I grab a cup from a shelf, and quickly fill it with coffee from the machine. I'm sitting at the table, adding the fixings, when Dolly walks into the room and stares at me. "Hi Dolly." I give her a bright smile. "I was just heading to the library when I smelled the coffee. Do you want a cup?"

"No, I'm fine. I've been searching the house for you. Mr. Harper told me you were in the library." She places one hand firmly under my arm. "I believe he'd like to speak to you. I'll carry the coffee."

She is silent as she escorts me back to the library. I make myself comfortable in the chair by the window and Dolly closes the door as she leaves. Excitement shivers through me at the thought of seeing Alex again. It's not as if I have any romantic notions toward him. It's never been like that between us. We just like each other's company. I sip my coffee and realize having John so close is disturbing me and I really don't know why. Maybe it's a second sense that is warning me of danger? The argument we had before the accident must have been bad for me to run away. I wonder where I was going? Where did I wreck the SUV and why didn't John come after me? So many questions and they're all locked inside my head. I wonder if they will ever emerge out of the fog?

My thoughts are broken by the creaking of the heavy oak door. My stomach squeezes as I see John standing in the doorway. His expression is as composed as normal but I see a flicker of unease in his eyes. As he steps into the room, the familiar scent of his cologne reaches me and mingles with the musty aroma of old books and polished wood. I peer at him over the rim of my cup.

"Jessie. We need to talk." He closes the door firmly behind him and takes the chair opposite mine.

It's surreal that this man that I love with all my heart and know so intimately is little more than a stranger. It's as if I'm seeing him through someone else's eyes, as if our life together never existed. As if it's been one long dream—or maybe a nightmare. I smile at him. "I'd love to talk to you, John. I'm so lonely here and I miss my home. It's very nice here, and I appreciate you moving me from a sterile hospital room but I want to go home. I want to be with you and the girls."

"I know it's difficult for you and it's hard on me too." He shakes his head. "It's not that."

He appears conflicted and John is the most decisive man I know. I sigh. "If it's about the papers, I've already told you, John, I'm not signing. I've spoken to Mr. Collins and he agrees with me that I need more time before I make important decisions. By signing them now, they could easily be challenged in court. I have memory loss. It might never come back but I need to give it time. Mr. Collins said I can take all the time I need."

"This isn't just about the papers, Jessie." He runs a hand

through his hair, his agitation evident. "It's about us and everything that's happened. We need to talk it out. Since you woke up, it's as if the problems between us have magnified. Look, I know I'm not perfect but if we can discuss what's troubling you, we can start afresh."

A surge of anger shimmers through me. I have so many unanswered questions they are suffocating me. "How about we start with the reason you turned off my life support?"

"The doctors told me you were gone, Jessie." A shadow passes over his features and his face tightens. "They said that your brain function was minimal and, if you survived, you'd be a vegetable. I couldn't stand to see you suffer a moment longer." He leans forward, cradling his head in his hands. "The doctors told me you'd recover after the induced coma so I insisted on many procedures to make you look the same. You'd suffered significant facial damage in the wreck. I did this so you'd be happy. After the last one you didn't recover as expected. It was my fault for trying to make you perfect again. I only did it because I care for you."

He didn't mention the word "love" and I finish my coffee as if what he's saying is having no effect on me. I keep my voice low and civil. I don't want to fight with him but I need to get my point across or this discussion is useless. "They obviously made a mistake, didn't they? It was too soon after the wreck to make a decision like that. Brain-dead is dead, low brain function is alive. I was in there fighting and you didn't even give me a chance to recover, and we discussed this in length when we married. I made it quite clear that I valued life. You disrespected my wishes."

"I'm sorry, Jessie." John reaches out a hand to me and then drops it. "I don't know what to say."

I fix my gaze on him. I feel tears running down my cheeks. I don't want to cry. "Tell me the truth, John. I was just a burden to you, wasn't I? You sent me here to die so you didn't have to look at me."

"No! I did it because I love you. I couldn't stand seeing you like that." He looks at me, his eyes pleading. "I blame myself for the accident." He narrows his gaze. "Do you remember anything at all about that night?"

I shake my head. "Only hitting the tree, and that's a muddle of bad dreams and reality. I'm slowly remembering things that happened. I know I was taking art classes and I met a writer named Alex. I recall confronting my father over my grandma's letter; from then on it gets a bit fuzzy. I don't have any recollection of an argument with you. I know we had one but what it was about eludes me right now. Do you want to fill in the blanks?"

"I can't." John leans forward in his chair. "I've spoken to Dolly today and she said the doctor is very happy with your progress but insists you should try and recall what happened." He stands and moves his chair closer; he sits and takes my hands. "He said he could try hypnosis. Sometimes it helps but remembering naturally is the best thing. So I declined the offer."

I meet his gaze. "See, you're making decisions without asking me. I'm your wife, John, not a child or a pet. I need to know what happened. I would have agreed to the hypnosis. I want to get my life back and come home. I need my family. I *need* you."

"That can't happen, not yet." John drops my hands. "Not until I'm sure you're fully recovered. I can't care for you while I'm working. It's best that you're here with Dolly."

I want to get angry and slap his face but he looks so tragic. He just doesn't understand. "I don't want to be here with Dolly. She won't tell me anything. She doesn't discuss anything with me apart from what I like to eat. Every time I bring up the girls, she changes the subject just like you do. Why won't you tell me about the girls?"

"It's complicated." John stares at the thick plush carpet as if unable to meet my scrutiny. "Your exact memory of what happened that night right up until the wreck is crucial to what happens next." He lifts his gaze slowly. "It's not just me and the doctors who need to know what happened. The cops are involved and it's taken moving you here in secrecy to keep them off your back. The doctor is protecting you to some degree but it won't last forever. Once they know you've regained consciousness, they'll be here on the doorstep, demanding details, which you obviously can't give them."

I stare at him. "The cops are involved? I hadn't been drinking. It was just an accident." I grip his arm and squeeze hard, my nails pressing into the skin beneath his shirt. "Why is that? Did I kill someone?"

My head spins at the implications. Did I kill my girls? Is that why nobody will talk about them? A pain stabs at my head like a strike of lightning as a flashback penetrates my mind. I'm suddenly there inside my shiny bright red SUV. I'm trembling with anger and the vehicle is weaving across the road. Someone is shouting at me and I'm screaming back at them. A hand closes around the steering wheel and aims me at a tree. I'm fighting to gain control but it's useless. I'm living my nightmare.

"Jessie." John is shaking me. "Jessie, what's wrong? Do you remember something?"

I taste blood in my mouth as I open my eyes. My lip is sore from biting it. Someone was in the car with me and caused the accident. Who was it? I look into John's expression of concern and shake my head. I don't trust him. Is he worried about me remembering who was in the vehicle? What if it was him? Why the big cover-up? Did he try to kill me? The reason he flicked the switch on my ventilator suddenly made sense: His affair with Ms. Lawson, and my massive inheritance. He is unaware that I changed my will, and he'd assume the old wills we made together still stand and as my husband my estate would go to him. Everything points to him wanting to get his hands on my money.

I massage my temple willing the scene in my head to return. I need to concentrate on the hand clamped on the wheel but the memory fades as fast as it arrived. I look at John. He claims he wasn't with me that night. Is he lying? "I'm sorry. I get sharp pains in my head but they pass quickly. I'm fine. Now tell me why the cops are involved."

"I'm not allowed to discuss anything about that night, Jessie. Including what the cops want to speak to you about." John blows out a breath in frustration and runs a hand down his face. "I blame myself for the accident. I did something stupid—I know that now." A sound like a wounded animal escapes his lips. "When the doctors couldn't discover any reason why you were in a coma and said it was as if you'd given up the will to live, I went ballistic."

I reach for my coffee and sip the lukewarm brew. "I'm not surprised. Everything that was going on in the months before the wreck was traumatic. I remember most of it. You not coming home for days on end, and flaunting Ms. Lawson in my face."

"How could you say such a thing?" John leans back in his chair and his expression hardens. "Rebecca is my lawyer. I need her at the meetings when I make deals with clients. Taking responsibility for people's investments in the market has legal ramifications." He shakes his head. "You've always had it in for her, haven't you? Maybe if you tried to get to know her, you will see she is no threat to you."

I shake my head and tears sting my eyes. "I've seen the way you look at her and the way you talk to her, I'm not stupid or blind."

"Jessie, please, you need to believe me; there's nothing going on between us." John grabs my hands. "I've never been unfaithful to you."

Lies pour from his mouth and I drag my hands away from him and wrap my arms around my chest. My cheeks are wet with tears and I try desperately to hold back the sobs threatening to break free. "So many things have happened between us. How do you expect me to believe you anymore? Everything that comes from your lips sounds like a lie."

"I know things have been difficult, Jessie, but I'm here now and I want to make things right." Desperation creeps into his voice and he gives me his best hangdog expression.

Right now nothing he says will work. I'm angry for the hell he put me through. I was never worthy of his love until I inherited the estate. "What do you mean by 'make things right'? You turned off my life support and now you want to control my inheritance. How can I ever trust you again?"

"Let me stay here tonight, Jessie." Determination flashes in his eyes. "I want to be here for you to prove that you can trust me."

I've wanted him to say that for so long. My resolve wavers but the doubts and fears are too strong. "Not yet, I need time to figure things but I do want you to visit me more often. Seeing you is unlocking my memories and, good or bad, we should face them together."

"I'll come by as often as possible." John stood and then bent to brush a kiss over my cheek, like he would his mother. "Just don't shut me out. Don't forget I was there that night and I'll be able to help you sort through the memories once they start emerging."

He left, closing the door softly behind him. I sink back into the armchair, despair and exhaustion washing over me. As his footsteps disappear along the passageway, the empty room fills with the ghosts of doubts and unanswered questions. I can't trust John yet. Not until my mind unlocks all the answers I need. Our conversation spins around in my head. It's been twelve months since the wreck and the cops still want to speak to me. Why? I lost control and hit a tree. I search my mind. Someone was in the car with me—or is that just part of my nightmare? If I was alone, apart from my girls, in the car that night, who did I kill? I push my knuckles into my mouth to stop the scream. The reason no one will mention the twins slams into me. I killed my girls.

TWENTY-SIX

3 MONTHS BEFORE THE ACCIDENT

The feeling of being followed refuses to leave me. I'm constantly on my guard, doing what comes close to rituals before I leave the house. I walk through each room and peer through the windows to check no one is outside. My neck prickles as the garage door slides open. He's out there, I can feel eyes on me. I hide behind my sunglasses to scan the blacktop both ways before driving out of my garage. I know I'm not imagining things when the same truck pulls away from the curb and follows, keeping a few vehicles behind. Who is this person and why are they following me?

Acutely aware of my tail, I park outside the local bookstore. I'm enjoying reading Alex's series and head inside to browse the shelves. I love the shop, it has the scent of aged paper and coffee. The owner has a little coffee corner and sells sweet buns and barista coffee. Most people in the store are like I am, scanning the shelves or making purchases, but then I feel eyes on me. The intuition is so strong it's almost like a touch. I don't want to look over my shoulder, so I peer into the reflection in the store window. A man is standing a few aisles away, pretending to flip through a magazine, but his attention is fixed on me. Men look at me from time to time and I want to brush it off but, as I move to the counter, I see him readying himself to follow me. I'm trembling as I take my credit card from my purse. The bell above the door chimes and I glance up to see the man leaving the shop, taking in every detail of his appearance. Should I report him to the cops—no, I have no proof that he is actually following me. I haven't even got his license plate.

Maybe I'm just imagining it? They say stress does strange things and with all that's going on in my life right now, it's not surprising part of me would break sooner or later. I wish I could discuss my fears with John that some time ago I heard something or someone moving in the house. It always seemed to happen when John was away. He'd come home and I'd tell him. He'd walk around and check the windows and doors and tell me I was imagining things. When I insisted, he looked me straight in the eye and told me if I didn't pull myself together, he'd hire someone to care for the children, because he didn't trust me alone with them. The noises continued and it wasn't until I mentioned it to a friend at the tennis club and she recommended a pest control guy, that I discovered I had a racoon living in my roof.

I wasn't imagining the noises then and the feeling of being watched is still there. It's like a rash crawling over me. As I pull out from the curb, I check the rearview mirror. The truck is back. My heart misses a beat and I'm hyperventilating. I need to know, one way or another, and go through my usual routine. I drive erratically, turning left and right, and racing through red lights. I check my mirror and he's not behind me. I turn back onto Main and head home. I take another look in the mirror. Fear grips my belly, and my hands tighten on the steering wheel.

He's back.

Dare I tell John? Will he figure I'm delusional or will he believe me this time? I shake my head. He won't believe me, I know it. I have nothing, no proof this is happening to me. The thing is, the man following me is a different type of pest. This one I can see.

I'm now dashing from place to place and making sure I'm never alone. My nerves are in shreds and I only feel safe in the art studio. I join a morning session, glad to see Alex at his easel. "You're almost finished. Will you start another?"

"Yeah, this place is a goldmine for my mental brainstorming." Alex flicks his brush over the canvas. "My book is with my publisher and I'm researching the next one. Being here a few times a week is beneficial in more ways than one. I'm actually selling my paintings." He gives me a wide grin. "I feel like celebrating, how about lunch at the new bistro?" He pulled out his phone. "I'll book a table. Around one okay for you?"

I smile back. "Congratulations, and yes, I'd love to come. I'll dash home and change and meet you there."

I finish up early and I'm excited as I hurry to my vehicle. My heart sinks at the sight of a white truck parked alongside the road. I look at the distinctive grill and make a mental note of the small blue sticker on the front bumper. I swallow hard. Is it the same truck? How can I be sure? My palms are sweaty as I grip the steering wheel, now too afraid to peer into the rearview mirror in case he's there. Panic shivers through me as I take a peek. The truck is there, same as before, two vehicles back. I park in the garage and lock the door behind me. I need to be back with people. No one would attack me in a public place, would they?

I rush to dress and then drive way too fast to the bistro, leave my SUV in the parking lot, and then head inside. I turn before I push open the door and see the truck slipping into a bay a few vehicles away from my red SUV. It sits among the other vehicles like a red thumb. I couldn't hide if I wanted to. I catch a glimpse of my reflection in the window. I look terrified and try to calm my expression before I walk inside.

The new place has a lovely homey atmosphere, with a variety of exotic dishes. I inhale air infused with the aroma of spices. I see Alex at once and he rises as I join him. We peruse the menu, discussing the dishes and deciding to get a few to share. I give the server my order and freeze as she walks away. The man from the bookstore is sitting in the corner with his gaze on me. Chills run down my spine at the sight of him. I turn to look at Alex and smile. "I know you're going to think I'm crazy but see that guy sitting in the corner? I believe he's been following me for the last couple of weeks." I describe the truck.

"Is it every time you go out or only when you meet me?" Alex tore open a bread roll and added butter from a dish on the table.

I think for a beat. "Both… well, I think so, anyway. I was heading for the art studio this morning and before that he was watching me at the bookstore." I meet his gaze. "He's just sitting there, staring at me. It's unnerving."

"It might be a coincidence." Alex smiles. "Surely you're used to men looking at you?"

I shrug. "No not really. I'm just a mom."

"Well, forgive me for saying but you're beautiful." He holds up both hands. "And I'm not hitting on you. I'm just stating a fact. The other thing, the truck you described, let's face it, there are hundreds of them here."

I sigh and stare at the plate of delicious food the server places before me. "You're probably right." I indicate to the door. "He just left."

A wave of relief washes over me. Perhaps I'm a victim of an overactive imagination. I guess time will tell.

TWENTY-SEVEN

NOW

Something isn't right. My limbs are heavy and I can hardly keep my eyes open. I'm sure Dolly is drugging me. After my shower, she came in all cheery with a cup of hot chocolate with marsh-mallows floating on the top. I peer at the remnants of the drink on the nightstand, glad that I didn't finish it. It didn't taste right and I only had a few mouthfuls, so whatever she put in it was powerful enough to knock me out fast. I rack my brain, trying to come up with some reason why she'd want to do this to me. I'm not hysterical; in fact, we had a long talk after John left. I didn't say too much but it was as if she already knew what we'd discussed. She even mentioned the argument I had with John the night of the accident. I told her I didn't recall what it was about only that there was an argument. Now I know something is terribly wrong because the only person who could have told her is John. Are they working together to make me appear to be unstable? Greed makes people do terrible things, so it's possible.

When she questioned me earlier, I was so careful to hide my feelings, so why is she drugging me? What the heck is happening? She is supposed to be helping me. I try to make my muddled brain work and the only conclusion I come up with is she needs me out of the way for a few hours. What the heck is she planning?

My attention moves to the camera; it's a simple nanny cam placed on a shelf opposite the end of my bed. I hate being under observation all the time. Being watched is horrible, and trust me, I haven't forgotten being followed in the months before the accident. There are many things I remember that I will not reveal to anyone. Some things are best kept private. I grit my teeth, determined to disable that camera. The room spins around me as I cling to the edge of the bed. With heavy legs I make it to the nightstand and force myself to keep moving. Each step takes momentous effort but I'm determined to win. My vision blurs as I stumble toward the small camera. I know when she's looking at me, the red light on the front blinks and it's not blinking now. My hands shake as I take hold of it and rip it from the wall. I carry it like a trophy back to the bed and then drop it into the compartment below the seat in my walker.

A door in the passageway opens and closes. Panic grips me as I crawl into bed, my body heavy and uncooperative. I drag the covers over me and pretend to be asleep. My pulse is thumping so fast in my ears I have to strain to hear. Muffled footsteps approach and Dolly enters the room. She's speaking to someone on the phone and her voice is low and urgent.

"She's starting to remember the argument with you. What do you want me to do?" She sighs. "She's asleep. No, she can't overhear me. I've given her enough medication to knock her out for eight hours. Likely she'll forget all about the argument by morning."

I try to keep my breathing even but inside I'm in mental turmoil. The woman I thought was a caring friend is working against me and the only person she could be talking to is John. I clamp down hard on my jaw, my mind racing. Why is John doing this? What are they hiding from me? The drugs try to pull me under but anger is spiking my adrenaline. I'm fighting to stay awake. I need to piece together the fragments of my shattered reality. Dolly's voice fades as she leaves the room, leaving me alone with my thoughts.

She betrayed me but I'm stronger than they imagine.

I'll find out the truth, no matter the cost.

TWENTY-EIGHT

2 MONTHS BEFORE THE ACCIDENT

Although I'm trying to push the horrible feeling of being followed to the back of my mind, I'm still seeing the truck and glimpses of the man I'm convinced is following me, and my paranoia grows stronger every day. I love being at the art studio. The smell of fresh paint and the sounds of brushes on canvas are usually a comfort and I try desperately to lose myself in my creation but the truck was behind me again today after I dropped the girls at school and now my nerves are on edge. No amount of deep breathing or distraction will free me from the fear. I'm convinced this guy is just biding his time to attack me or the girls.

As I squeeze aquamarine onto my pallete, I glance up. There's a man lurking in the garden outside the studio. My heart races and I struggle to focus on the vibrant colors in front of me. Suddenly I'm trapped in a waking nightmare, unable to escape. I can't breathe, the room is closing in around me. I take a step closer to Alex and stare sightless at his painting. I lower my voice to just above a whisper. "Alex, that man. The one from the bistro who's been following me. He's outside in the garden."

"This is getting out of hand." Alex puts down his palette and brush and heads out of the door.

I hold my breath as he walks straight up to the man. They talk for a time and then shake hands. When he comes back into the studio, I turn to him. "What did he say?"

"He's the new landscape gardener for the estate." Alex smiles at me. "He's been working in your area, so that's why you've seen him hanging around. He seems like a nice enough guy. I don't figure he's stalking you."

I sigh with relief. "Oh, that's good to know."

It's funny but after Alex spoke to him, nobody followed me home.

I need to stay positive, so this week, I'm trying to live a normal life. I've pushed John's antics to the back of my mind and stepped away from any involvement with the mysterious other family. Instead, I went to my grandmother's house and helped Mom pack up Grandma's clothes and we sent them to Goodwill. My grandma had often spoken to us about what to do when she, as she would put it, "left the building" and keeping busy is helping to some degree. Maybe Alex is right and I'm just oversensitive about people going about their day-to-day lives. I want to believe it's over but it's only two days since Alex spoke to the man in the studio garden, and another vehicle is following me as I drive to the tennis club. I try to fight it but paranoia creeps back into my life like an unwelcome friend.

I complete my usual maneuvers, just to be sure, but there he is, following me around the block. I stop at the curb and he drives past me and pulls in just ahead. I stare at his vehicle, convinced he's going to get out, walk toward me, and shoot me or something. Panic grips me and I grab my phone and, hands trembling, I call John. I know he hates me disturbing him at the office but I have no choice.

"What is it, Jessie? I'm on my way to a meeting."

I sink down low in my seat trying to hide and fix my attention on the driver's door waiting for it to open. "There's a man following me. It's been happening for the last couple of weeks. He followed me to the bookstore, the bistro, and the art studio. I'm on my way to the tennis club and he's been tailing me since I left home." The phone slips in my sweaty palms. "I don't know what to do."

"Why would someone want to follow you? Jessie, you're just being paranoid." He blows out a sigh. *"I'm sure it's just a coincidence. It's a gated community; it's not like we have serial killers lurking around."*

His complete lack of compassion stings. "It's not a coincidence. He's always there watching me."

"Jessie, you need to calm down." His footsteps come through the speaker and the sound of a door closing. He's obviously too embarrassed to let anyone hear our conversation. *"You're letting your imagination get the better of you. We've spoken about this before, haven't we? Maybe we need to go to the doctor and explain. Maybe he can refer you to a psychologist or give you some meds to calm you down."*

I need support and he dismisses me as if I don't matter. "It's not my imagination. I can see him right now."

"Look, I can't deal with this right now." I hear the squeak of the wheels on John's office chair; he's obviously at his desk. *"I have a meeting, we'll talk about it later."* He disconnects.

I stare at the phone in my hand with a mixture of anger and helplessness. Why didn't he believe me? Why is he always so dismissive? I start the engine and complete a J-turn and go back the way I came. I keep my eye on the rearview mirror, but no one is following. Is the man real or am I losing my grip on reality? I know it's not the same man as before but then why are two different men following me? My mind races with questions. As I drive, I use the Bluetooth to call Alex. "I know you're going to believe I'm losing my mind but someone is following me again and it's not the same person as it was before." I clear my throat waiting for the same reaction as I received from John. "Can you think of any reason why someone would follow me?"

"You're speaking to an author who writes mysteries, so yeah, I can come up with a hundred reasons why people could be following you." Alex sounds concerned. *"Can you put a time-frame on when this first happened?"*

I nod as if he's sitting beside me. "Yes, about a week or so after I joined the art classes."

"Ah, I see." Alex clears his throat *"Give me a few minutes; I need to look into something. I'll call you right back."* He ends the call.

When I arrive home, the housekeeper is in the kitchen, preparing the evening meal. She'd collected the girls from school and they are playing in their room. I go and see them and then head into the office and close the door behind me. A few minutes passes before Alex calls me back. "Did you find out anything?"

"Yes, unfortunately I did." His tone is solemn. *"The new landscape gardener doesn't exist. I called the community manager's office and they don't have a new gardener. Add the fact that this started after you met me. I figure, you're being followed by two private detectives. I'd say, someone believes we're having an affair."*

Speechless, I'm unable to utter a word. "Why would John believe I'm having an affair?"

"Have you done anything different to make him think so?" Alex sounds interested.

I hate to admit I'm having problems in my marriage but I trust Alex. "John is never home. He spends most of his time in his apartment in town. I very rarely see him. I became so lonely that I moved into the spare room. I couldn't stand having the empty space beside me night after night and not knowing if he was spending his time with Ms. Lawson."

"Does he know you're sleeping in the spare room?"

I stare at my reflection in the mirror, I've lost weight and have dark circles beneath each eye. "Yes. He came home twice very late but didn't say a word. I don't believe he noticed I was missing."

"Oh, he noticed." There's a rasping sound as Alex scratches his beard. *"Then I show up with you when you go to see your father. So he decided to find out rather than confronting you. I imagine he is very confused at the moment, because there can't be any proof whatsoever that we're more than acquaintances. The next time he decides to come home, maybe you should ask him why he has sent private detectives after you. If he mentions me in the conversation, maybe you should remind him that you're allowed to have friends and not every friend is a lover."*

Anger flares. "I called him at work today and told him someone was following me and he told me I should see a shrink." I shake my head in disbelief. "When all the time he sent the men to follow me. What kind of husband does that to someone they're supposed to love?"

"A very jealous one, I'd say." Alex sighs *"I have an instant solution that won't affect our friendship. Just tell him I'm gay."*

Suddenly a great weight lifts from my shoulders and I laugh like a loon. "Alex, you're the best friend I've ever had."

"My pleasure. I'll see you at the studio tomorrow. I'll be there by nine. Sleep well." He disconnects.

Everything Alex said fits. I'm being manipulated and the sad thing is it's by my own husband.

TWENTY-NINE

1 MONTH BEFORE THE ACCIDENT

John has been coming home every night for the last two weeks. Not that I see much of him as he gets in around ten, showers, and then falls into bed and goes to sleep. I haven't been able to broach the subject of him hiring a private detective to follow me. Although, I'm not so afraid of them now and make a point of ignoring them but they're still there. I decide to sit up and wait for him. We need to have this out once and for all. A key turns in the lock and John comes into the kitchen. He does a double take when he sees me sitting at the table, nursing a cup of coffee. "There you are. Have you eaten? Can I get you anything?"

"Coffee would be nice. I'm not hungry; I grabbed a meal at the bistro." John drops his briefcase on a chair and sits down opposite me. "I didn't expect to see you waiting up for me."

I push a cup of coffee in front of him with two sugars and cream just as he likes it. "I never see you lately so this is the only time I'll get a chance to speak to you."

"Okay." John's blue eyes move over me and his lips twitch into a sardonic smile. "So what's this all about? Do you want a divorce?"

His words shock me and it must show on my face. "Do I have a reason to ask you for a divorce?"

"Well, considering you've been sleeping in the spare room for the last two months, I figure something must be up." He leans back in his chair; one hand rests on the table the manicured fingers drumming. "It's hardly a friendly environment, is it?"

I raise my eyebrows and stare at him. "I moved into the spare room because I couldn't stand not feeling you on the opposite side of the bed. You're never home and I didn't even know until Michael told me that you had an apartment in Manhattan and you stay there frequently overnight."

"I honestly didn't think you'd be interested in what I do overnight." He shrugs and looks past me through the window and then turns his gaze slowly back to me. "FYI, I've taken on a number of international portfolios and it means I need to take phone calls at all hours of the night. Up to this week that is, I managed to convince the boss to hand them over to the unmarried partner. I told him it was not working out for us with me away all the time. He actually agreed. So if you don't want a divorce what's on your mind?"

I sip my coffee and look at him over the rim. It's hard to believe he's been at work all day. Apart from his tie, which he loosened when he sat down, he doesn't have a hair out of place. His clothes never have a wrinkle. I'll never understand how he does it. "Do you recall me mentioning that someone has been following me?"

"Vaguely." John grasps his cup, his large hand dwarfing it. "Why?"

I shake my head. "You know why, John. There are two different men and two different vehicles. It's been going on for a long time and not one of them has tried to hurt me or cause me any problems. I've spoken to a number of people about this and they all come to the same conclusion."

"Which is?" John places his cup on the table and his mouth flattens into a straight line.

I smile at him, as if I've caught him in a lie. "That they're private detectives, and you likely asked them to follow me because you believe I'm having an affair. I'm not sure why you would think such a thing but it's the only explanation." I lean forward and stare at him. "Are you having me followed?"

"Of course I'm having you followed." John slams his fist down hard on the table. "You showed at my office with another man. You've been out to lunch with him, you meet him at the art studio." He leans forward, his eyes boring into me. "You're sleeping in the spare room. What do you expect me to believe? I need to know the truth because, as sure as hell, I'll never get it from you."

I jerk back as if he's slapped my face. "I've explained why I've been sleeping in the spare room and Alex is a friend I met at the art studio. He is nothing more than a friend, which you would have discovered by now." I point a finger at him. "You were never home and that's why I joined the art studio because I was lonely and sick of listening to the gossip at the tennis club. That doesn't mean I went out and had an affair with the first man I met. Another thing, you can't pick my friends and whether they're male or female is irrelevant. I can assure you, there is no attraction between me and Alex. He's more like a brother to me."

"I figured you were getting back at me because of Rebecca." John sips his coffee and his eyes dart back and forth. "I know you're jealous of her."

Heat rises from my neck and up into my cheeks. "Why would I be jealous of her? I'm the one married to you. Or have you done something you're ashamed of? I'm sure there's something in your contract of employment that prohibits you from having affairs with your subordinates."

"I could talk to you until I'm blue in the face and you'd

never believe that I wasn't having an affair with Rebecca." He dashes a hand through his hair. "I know we spend a lot of time together but I've only ever once gone to her apartment, and she's never come to mine. I've never given her the address."

I snort, suddenly finding what he was saying hilarious. "At least she knows you have an apartment. I guess telling me slipped your mind, huh?"

"It's irrelevant." John shrugs. "The company purchased it for me because it was cheaper than living out of hotel rooms. I've set up an office there, so I can work overnight and catch some sleep in between. That's not something I can do at work."

If he's lying, he's covering up very well. I can't spot one iota of guile in his expression. "They gave you a Manhattan apartment? I find that hard to believe."

"It's a tax write-off." John smiles. "I'd be stupid to refuse. It's a good investment." He stretches his hand across the table and his warm palm closes around my fingers. "I'll call off the P.I.s if you move back into our bedroom. I've been sleeping alone for the last few months and I don't want to do it in my own home." He looks at me and his eyes soften. "I love you. Let's put all this behind us and start afresh."

He looks so genuine but then he has that charm that can convince anyone of anything. He would have made a great car salesman but he hasn't convinced me he isn't involved with Ms. Lawson. I refuse to think of her as Rebecca. When he uses her name, the way it rolls off his tongue sounds too intimate. "I love you too but you're making it hard to keep forgiving you, John." I narrow my gaze at him. "Don't you understand how I feel? Not telling me about the apartment makes me feel irrelevant but I'm glad you've admitted to having people follow me. I wish you'd told me the day I called you. I'm sure you can't imagine how terrifying it is, believing that someone intends to do you harm. You could have stopped that immediately but you didn't. Call off your goons and then I'll move back into our bedroom." I pull my hand from his grasp. "Goodnight, John."

My legs tremble as I climb the stairs, and inside my room I lean against the door. All the time I've been terrified someone was following me, John knew I was scared, and did nothing. He was more intent on finding some dirt on me than my well-being. A husband is meant to be your best friend, and yet I've found more compassion and friendship from a stranger than I ever have with John in all the time we've been married. Although I have to admit, he's changed since my inheritance. I'm starting to believe it's the only reason he married me. Although we survived the first few rough years when it was obvious he couldn't settle down with one woman, he had changed for the better until Ms. Lawson came into our lives. I'm not stupid, and even a blind person can see how much he admires her. The way he looks at her is the same way he looked at me once and his fascination with her is even more evident in the photographs on her social media pages. Now he's changed again. It's as if he realizes I might be worth my weight in gold after all.

THIRTY

NOW

My head is muddled, and my mouth is so dry my tongue sticks to the roof. I grab the bottle of water on the bedside table and empty it. As the water gushes down my throat, my head starts to clear. The conversation Dolly had with someone on the phone comes back with crystal clarity and so is the memory of speaking to Alex. He would come by later and I'll ask him about what happened before the accident and what we did together, in the hope it might jog my memory. I can't stop thinking about the note that Maria gave me, telling me not to trust anyone. Who sent it and how did they know what was happening to me? If they cared enough to leave a warning, why hadn't they tried to stop Dolly and John?

Nothing is making sense right now. I climb out of bed and reach for my walker but I'm getting stronger now and don't need it so much. I lift up the top of the seat and see the camera inside. I grab my clothes, drape them over the walker, and head for the bathroom. This time I lock the door. The camera is small and fits in my palm. I turn it over staring at it with contempt. Has Dolly been recording my every move and my emotions to use against me? The idea sickens me. Dammit I trusted her. I look around but there's no suitable place to hide it, so I wrap it in toilet paper and flush it. It's satisfying to see it vanish into the sewer. I spend a long time under the shower, the flow of water helps remove the residue fuzziness in my head. Once I'm dressed, I sit on the seat of my walker to dry my hair and apply makeup. Surely if I wasn't in control of my faculties, as everyone is trying to make me believe, I wouldn't care what I look like, would I?

I don't want to eat alone, so make my way slowly to the kitchen, where I find Maria making breakfast. I don't have any reason not to trust her; in fact, she might be my only ally in the house. I sit down with a steaming cup of coffee before me. I've chosen a seat where I can watch the door and, as Maria busies herself making hot cakes, I try to act casual. "Have you discovered anything more about that note that you found addressed to me?"

"Only this morning. I was going to tell you when I brought you your breakfast." Maria turns to look at me over one shoulder. "I doubt you would know but many of the gardeners lost their jobs when your grandmother died. So they don't tend the gardens daily as before. I spoke to the one who gave me the note this morning. He said it was your brother Michael who gave him the note and asked him to leave it on the table."

Unable to believe my ears, I stare at her. "But Michael isn't here. He's overseas. When was the note left for me?"

"It was the week before you regained consciousness." Maria's eyebrows met in a frown. "I kept it in my pocket because the gardener said it was to go to no one else but you."

Nodding, I stare at my coffee. As far as I knew, Michael had been overseas. "Did anyone in the house mention to him that I was waking up?"

"Not that I'm aware." Maria piles pancakes on a plate, adds crispy bacon, and hands me a warm bottle of maple syrup. "No one talked to me about you until you woke up and needed meals." She refills my coffee cup. "Although I hear Dolly talking about you on the phone, all the time. She gives everyone updates on your condition."

I nod. "Don't tell her about the note. I need you to contact my brother's office and leave a message that, the moment he comes back, I need to speak to him." I indicate to the pen and notebook on the counter. "Pass me the notebook and I'll write down his details. Don't tell anyone. There's another thing. My friend Alex might visit. If you see him, don't tell anyone, okay?"

"Yes, of course." Maria nods. "I'm good at keeping secrets."

I finish my meal, fill two travel mugs with coffee, and wedge them inside my walker seat before heading toward the conservatory. I look over one shoulder at Maria. "I haven't seen Dolly today. If she comes searching for me, tell her I'm in the conservatory getting some sun." If she finds me there with Alex, it's just too bad.

Time drags by. Nine seems so far away but I'm enjoying the peace of this place. It's all marble, with ornate columns and a huge expanse of glass. It is essentially a massive greenhouse, although with the addition of comfortable furniture including a table and chairs. Plants fill the space and give the air a damp quality, like walking in the forest after the rain. The mingled scents of the flowering shrubs and hanging baskets overflowing with flowers are as delightful as the sight. The colors are intense, purples, pinks, bright orange, and red, spread out like an artist's palette. The comparison immediately reminds me of Alex, and his hilarious antics in the art studio. He had everyone laughing most of the time with his stories.

As if on cue, Alex emerges from the pathway through the rose bushes. When he sees me, a wide grin splits his face. I smile back, suddenly conscious of my pathetically thin body and sunken eyes. "Alex, how good to see you."

"I figured you needed someone to talk to." His gaze moves over me and he frowns. "Why are they keeping you isolated?

Surely familiar surroundings would help with your recovery?" He hands me a box of coffee creams from the little candy store in Grande Haven. They're my absolute favorites.

I hug the box to my chest and moan in appreciation. "Thank you." I nod toward the closed door leading to the rest of the house. "I agree, being at home would help but I don't believe they want me to get well." I went on to tell him my suspicions.

"You had concerns before the accident but you told me John was coming home more often and you were prepared to sort things out with him." Alex sat opposite, hands held loosely together between his knees. "What makes you figure they want to make you appear unstable?"

Memories flood my brain. "First, John having me followed and not telling me. Then the day after I regained consciousness a couple of women came by. I'm sure I don't know them although they acted like my friends, what they said made no sense whatsoever. Anyway, they said John had given all my things to Goodwill, but when I asked him to bring me something to wear he sent a few new things and Dolly said it was because I've lost weight." I sigh. "I don't know if he has cleaned out my things or not."

I went on to tell him about seeing my mom with the girls and the flowers in my room the next morning. I mention the ringing disconnected phone. I look at him as he assesses my story. "They kept me under video surveillance as well but I flushed the camera this morning."

"Heavens above, Jessie, I couldn't write this stuff." Alex rubs the back of his neck. "When I take into consideration everything you've told me, I believe the key to everything going on here is tied up in the night you had the car wreck. I've been thinking about that day as well, trying to piece together everything that happened before you went home. I recall you telling me that your housekeeper was going to collect the girls from school and so you stayed a little longer to finish."

The day falls into place and I nod. "Yes, I remember. Then what happened?"

"You took the painting home with you and we had to drape the back of the SUV with plastic sheets to prevent the paint damaging the upholstery." He pauses a beat. "Let me see. It was getting dark when you left but you did mention you'd be home before dinner. Can you remember what happened next?"

I dive into the seat of the walker and take out the two cups of coffee and hand him one. "I get bits and pieces. I recall most of the accident. Someone was screaming at me and there was a hand on the wheel. I'm sure whoever was in the car with me caused the accident. I recall fighting to keep the vehicle on the road, and someone was trying to push me into a tree. I remember the tree vividly; it had a jack-o'-lantern hanging from one of the branches."

"That's good because most people would forget the actual accident. That was the traumatic part of what happened to you." He scratches his cheek. "I've been to the library and hunted through the various reports of the accident. One of the tree branches smashed through the side window, and that's what cut your face. The report I read was quite informative, so I called the reporter and was able to speak to them. They actually went to the scene and looked at the SUV." Alex sucks in a deep breath and blows it out slowly. "Here's where it becomes strange. He said the airbags deployed but your head injury came from the right-hand side. The SUV wasn't damaged on the right-hand side at all. Nothing was said in any of the newspaper reports, but the reporter told me in confidence that in their opinion something or someone hit you from the right. You should have walked away from there with a few cuts on your face."

I swallow hard. The implications of what he's saying terrify me. "Do you figure they were trying to kill me and hit me hard enough to put me in a coma to make sure?"

"The thing is, you were trying to make things better between you and John. From what you've told me, it was John's idea." Alex sips his coffee. "So why would he want to spoil things? What reason does he have to want you dead or insane?"

Nodding slowly, I meet his gaze. "He has a reason. See this place? The house and the estate have been in my family for generations, add a substantial portfolio of shares and it adds up to my inheritance. Greed would be a reason, don't you figure?"

"Maybe but that would surely only involve the person who benefits from your will." Alex leans back in the chair. "How many people are we talking about?"

I nod, glad he understands. "Yes, I agree, and it's not John, but he doesn't know I made a new will, leaving him out at my grandmother's request. The person I left the estate to doesn't know either."

"So when you wrecked the car, John still believed he'd inherit everything?" Alex snorted. "That kinds of points the finger at him, don't you agree?"

The idea saddens me but I nod in agreement. "The thing is, my grandmother's will is still going through probate. It was almost through and then I had the accident. Yesterday, John tried to get me to sign a power of attorney, so he could manage the estate on my behalf. He actually brought Ms. Lawson to the meeting, even though he knows I hate her being near him. I don't trust her and I don't trust him with her, so I refused, saying I needed more time to recover before making such a momentous decision."

"Then what happened?" Alex places the travel mug on the table.

I lift my chin toward the door. "My nurse, Dolly, caught me in the kitchen just after I called you. Then the next thing I know my hot chocolate is drugged and I hear her talking on the phone about me. I believed I could trust her and now I know she's working for John." I search his face, willing him to believe me.

"So John inherits everything if you die? If you don't die and you're proved incompetent, he can take over the estate and run it on your behalf?" Alex narrows his gaze. "That would be a solid motive if I was writing a book." He rubs his chin observing me with interest. "But why now? When you're better and the estate passes into your control, you'll likely have John involved. Am I correct? If so, he doesn't have a motive."

I consider his argument. "Unless someone told him that I've changed my will." I bit my lip, not sure if I should divulge the secret. "Wouldn't that be a perfect motive for him to want power of attorney over me?"

"The thing is, Jessie." Alex meets my gaze. "It doesn't make sense if he were trying to make things right with you. I would have believed the opposite. Once you inherited, you'd probably hand over the running of the estate to him like I said before." He clasps his hands together. "It seems to me everything hinges on the night you had the accident. You had an argument with John and, from what I heard from your neighbors, you left the house in a hurry. What happened during that argument is crucial."

I stare at him blankly, trying to fit together a jumble of memories. "I don't remember."

"If John is living at home, your housekeeper would still be there, wouldn't she?" Alex smiles at me. "I'll visit her and see what information she has. Can you write me a note to give to her, I'm sure she would recognize your handwriting. I gather she's been with you for many years?"

Suddenly a ray of sunshine to pierce the fog in my brain. "What would I do without you, Alex?"

"I'd better go before Dolly discovers me here." Alex stands and shakes his head slowly. "It's a cruel joke they're playing but they don't know you have an ace up your sleeve. I'll be back as soon as I can. I'll check back here in three days' time. Stay strong."

I watch as he disappears into the roses and lean back in my chair. Fragments of memory slide into place. I see the face of Rebecca Lawson. Somehow, she's involved, I just know it. My mind goes back to the wreck; the hand on the steering wheel and the screaming in my ear can't just be in my head—can it? The nightmare and flashbacks are too real. As the newspaper reporter told Alex, if the car sustained no damage on the right side, how come my skull was fractured on that side? I recall the sudden blinding pain just before I hit the tree. My hands tremble as the horrible truth hits me. Whoever was in the car with me tried to murder me—and my girls. Was it John?

THIRTY-ONE

John surprises me with a visit, arriving a little after eight, carrying a large bag of popcorn under one arm, and his laptop under the other. It's not often I see John wearing casual clothes. His blue short-sleeved shirt is open at the neck and worn over a pair of bone-colored chinos. "I wasn't expecting you."

"I figured I'd surprise you." John leads me into the family room. "How about popcorn and a movie? I'm sure Maria can rustle us up a good bottle of wine."

I'm feeling a little insecure with him but at least he's making an effort. "I'd like that, thank you, but all the TVs have been removed, in case I see something disturbing that sends me crazy." I shake my head. "Although being in solitary confinement is more likely to do that than seeing something on the news."

"We can watch it on my laptop." John places the computer on the coffee table. "Don't worry too much. You're progressing so well I'm sure the doctor will allow you to watch TV soon."

I grab the opportunity while I can. "I've been remembering the night of the accident when we had that argument. I know it involved Ms. Lawson." I turn to him. "Look. I don't want to spoil our evening but I need to fit the pieces together so I can get well." I grip his arm. "She was there, wasn't she?"

"Yes, but only briefly." John's Adam's apple moves up and down as he scans my face. "I can't tell you anymore, Jessie. Allow it to come back on its own. You're not the only one who wants answers."

I lean back in the chair and close my eyes. "Yes, I know. The cops want to question me." I open my eyes and see his confusion. "There is one thing you can do for me."

"Anything." John takes my hand and rubs his thumb over the back.

It feels good to be touched but is he a snake waiting to bite? I don't know anymore. "Replace Dolly."

"I can't do that, on short notice." John runs a hand down his face. "She consults directly with your physician."

I knew he'd have an excuse but I have a good one of my own. "She's a palliative care nurse. I need someone who will actually spend time with me and that physical therapist you promised me. I want to get fit again."

"Okay, I'll see what I can do." He slips one arm around me. "Now let's watch the movie."

I rest my head on his shoulder and inhale his familiar cologne. It brings back wonderful memories of our time together. I want to sink into oblivion and just enjoy the moment but a little voice in my head is insistent. *Why is he being so nice?*

THIRTY-TWO

In the middle of the night, I'm not sure if I'm awake or asleep. Dreams cling to my reality and I sit up, shaking my head to rid myself of the disturbing images. Sweat coats me and my PJs cling to my cooling flesh. I put my head in my hands trying to extract the truth from the dream. Has my damaged mind decided to reveal itself when I'm asleep? I'm trembling but not in fear—I'm angry. I slide out of bed, grab a fresh nightgown, and push my walker into the bathroom. I lock the door and take a shower as the memory of the night of the accident slowly slots into place.

It's our wedding anniversary. The girls are asleep and I'm making salad to go with the steaks I purchased today from the market. John's voice comes from the hallway but he's not alone. I look up from the table as he comes into the kitchen with a wide grin on his face; behind him is Rebecca Lawson. She pokes him in the back and giggles. I'd looked from one to the other, waiting for an explanation. Who brings a lawyer to their anniversary dinner with their wife?

"Rebecca is moving into our guesthouse." John smiles as if

keeping his mistress on the grounds of our home and within a stone's throw of our children is perfectly normal.

I look from one to the other. Ms. Lawson is practically glowing. "I believe we need to discuss this in private."

"Don't be silly, Jessie, there's nowhere else for her to go. You know how difficult it is to get a place in Manhattan. Her apartment was damaged in the storm and it needs to be repaired. She's only going to be here for a week or so." John frowns at me and then turns on his heel. "I'll help her with her bags and then come back." He glances at the salad and raises an eyebrow. "Is there enough for three? If not, I'll take Rebecca to the bistro, we can worry about getting extra groceries tomorrow. It will be nice having company, won't it?"

Anger grips me, and I'm seeing red. How dare he bring that woman into my home? I somehow keep my voice low and in control. "Ms. Lawson, would you mind waiting outside while I speak to my husband, please?" I wait for her to go and when the front door clicks shut, I turn to John. "How dare you? You swore to me that you weren't having an affair with that woman and now you want to move her into our guesthouse—and on our anniversary? How gullible do you think I am? No woman in their right mind would agree to something like that. You can go and tell her to find a hotel because there is no way I'm staying in this house while she's here."

"I gave her my word." John looks taken aback. "Why are you making such a fuss over nothing? She's only going to be here a few months."

I toss the salad into the garbage, and glare at him. "In seconds it's gone from a couple of weeks to a few months." My heart is breaking as I turn to him. "It seems to me you've already made your choice."

"Oh, I have." John turns away from me and heads for the door. "She's staying."

I run for the stairs and throw clothes into suitcases, making sure I have enough for the girls, including a few of their favorite toys. I leave a note on our bed. I don't want him coming after me. It's over. I scribble a note:

I can't live like this any longer.

John has underestimated me. Before I inherited my grand-mother's house, I had nowhere to go and no money to support myself but, in a few weeks, the house will be transferred into my name and I will be a multimillionaire. I wake the girls gently and tell them we're going on vacation.

They're in the SUV, wrapped in blankets and safely secured, when John arrives. He tries to prevent me from getting into the car. "Let me go. If you think I'm staying here with her, then you are sadly mistaken. I *do* have some pride, you know."

"I won't let you." John yanks the door from my grasp. "Get back into the house. You're making a spectacle of yourself."

I push him hard in the chest. "If you don't let me go, I'll scream the place down and the neighbors will call the cops. Your face will be all over the Sunday paper by the time I finish telling my story. Get out of my way."

Before I can drive away, my brother arrives. I buzz down my window to speak to him. "I'm going to Grandma's house."

"Maybe we should talk before you go." Michael is eyeing me critically. "You need to calm down and think this through."

The memory from that point blurs into the dream I had about the accident. I don't remember John getting into the car and grabbing the wheel. Did I dream that part? No matter how angry I got I'd never speed with the girls in the vehicle. So how come I hit the tree? Confusion grips me. There's still one piece of the puzzle missing.

THIRTY-THREE

The next morning when Michael walks into the family room, my heart lifts. He looks just the same, well-dressed and fit. He is tanned and his smile looks whiter than ever. "Michael."

"I'm so happy to see you awake." He shakes his head and looks at me. "I'd hug you but I figure you might break."

I pat the sofa beside me; the plush velvet is soft and familiar under my palm. I'm desperate to find out about my girls but he's likely been told to withhold all information as well. I decide to start with something general. "Tell me all about your trip."

"It was business." Michael drops into the seat and shrugs. "Same old, same old, just in different settings. It was nice visiting other countries but I wanted to be here for you." He frowns. "John said there was no hope. I came by to see you a month ago but then the firm sent me overseas."

I nod. "You're here now. My memory is sketchy but it's coming back. I need to know everything that happened while I was in a coma."

"That's an entire year, Jessie." Michael rubs his chin. "Anything specific?"

"Do you know how long Ms. Lawson lived in my guesthouse?"

"As far as I know, she's still there." He frowns. "I believe she's living in the house now."

A cold chill crawls up my spine. John has spent time with me like he cares and all the while he's living with her. I swallow the bile crawling up my throat. "Really? John never mentions her. Not that I see him very often and then he's like a different person. He didn't seem very happy to see me awake."

"I don't believe he ever got over finding your suicide note." Michael shook his head. "I never understood why you wanted to end your life over Rebecca Lawson."

I stare at him in disbelief. I've never considered suicide. No wonder John has been so cold toward me for so long. I turn to Michael. "Suicide note? I never left a suicide note. So, he believes I deliberately ran into that tree?" *No wonder they won't allow me to see the girls. They believe I tried to kill them.*

"Yeah, I'm pretty sure." Michael scrubs a hand down his face. "I told him you'd never do such a thing."

I shake my head. "I left a note saying 'I can't live like this any longer' but I meant with *him*. I was heading here when I wrecked the car. I never did it on purpose. I'm surprised that John believes anything so ridiculous. Is that why the cops want to speak to me?"

"I don't know." Michael pushes a hand through his hair. "Don't get upset. I'll help you work everything out. You got my note, about not trusting anyone, didn't you? When John moved you here, I figured it was so you couldn't be resuscitated, so I left it in case you regained consciousness. That's when the firm sent me overseas. Likely John had a hand in it to keep me out of the way."

I stand and grab the walker. The truth is finally unravelling. "I did get your note but I only just found out it was from you." Flashbacks of the wreck hit my mind in lightning bolts. I need to change the subject before he notices something's wrong. "Did you know the house is closed up apart from the bottom floor?"

"Yeah, with no one here after Mom and Dad moved to Florida, it was the best thing to do." His gaze moves over me. "You okay, Jessie?"

I walk to the mantle and indicate to the photographs. I run my fingertips lovingly over the picture of my grandma. "There's been a few strange things happening here. Things I can't explain. First up, photographs are missing. All the family ones I remember are here. Do you know who moved them and why?"

"What are you talking about?" Michael grabs my shoulders. "What strange things and what missing photographs?"

I tell him about seeing Mom in the garden with the girls, the roses and then a dead phone ringing in the middle of the night. "So-called friends came to visit me and talked a load of crap. I didn't recognize them. I'm starting to believe John is trying to make people think I'm crazy so he can take over the estate. He tried to get power of attorney. I refused."

"I haven't spoken to John since he insisted on turning off your life support." Michael stares at me. His expression concerns me.

I step away, wanting to gauge his reaction. "Am I losing my mind?"

"Let's wind it back a bit." He searches my face. "I don't see any missing photographs."

I shake my head. "Remember the one I took at Christmas; you sat with the girls beside the tree and unwrapped the presents. You wore reindeer antlers and a red nose?"

"What girls?" He frowns. "Who are you talking about?"

Exasperated, I glare at him. "Okay, I know you're not allowed to talk about the girls, in case it makes me flip out. Did you get your orders too?"

"I don't know what you're talking about, Jessie. I haven't

spoken to anyone, apart from Dolly." Michael meets my gaze. He has a strange expression on his face. "She called the day you woke and I said I'd be home as soon as possible. When I asked after you, she told me you had memory loss but wasn't specific."

I sigh. "I can't remember everything about the accident but you know I'd never speed with the girls in the car. This is why no one will tell me about them, isn't it? They believe I tried to kill myself and take my girls with me." I feel his arms come around me. "You know I would never hurt them."

"No wonder John wants power of attorney. You need more time to get well, Jessie. You're not okay. The head trauma must have skewed your memory or you've been dreaming when you were in the coma." Michael stands me away from him, shaking his head. "I have no idea who has been feeding you these lies or why John hasn't sat you down and straightened you out. Maybe the doctors have spoken to him. I don't know."

I stare at him in disbelief. "What do you mean, straighten me out? What is everyone hiding from me that's so terrible it will send me crazy?" I glare at him. "Tell me or get out and never come back."

"You were pregnant with twins when you hit the tree. They didn't stand a chance." Michael holds me tight as if I might explode. "There are no girls, Jessie."

THIRTY-FOUR

THE NIGHT OF THE ACCIDENT

Anger shimmers through me as I climb behind the wheel of my red SUV. I head along the driveway and slow to watch John carrying luggage into our guesthouse. The light from the window spills out across the lawn and I can see the sitting room. He is inside with Ms. Lawson and she is kissing him on both cheeks and spinning around grinning as she surveys her new home. I want to spit, remembering the many hours I spent decorating the guesthouse to impress my visitors—not her, anyone but her. Seeing her there puts a bad taste in my mouth. I honestly feel like setting the place on fire rather than see her in it. Lights from a vehicle behind me blind me in the rearview mirror, and the next thing I know Michael is jumping into the passenger seat. He pulls up the top of his hoodie, as if he doesn't want anyone to recognize him. "If you're here to make me change my mind you won't be able to." I push my foot down hard on the gas and we flash through the entrance to my driveway and roar along the blacktop. "Are you sure you don't want to get out?" I head along Main and toward the gates of the estate.

"Nope, but I will make you see reason." Michael fastens his seatbelt. "You can slow down for a start."

I hit the highway and accelerate, but not any faster than the legal speed limit. The thing with Michael is that he can't get his head around the fact that women can drive as good as men. It will take me about an hour and twenty minutes to get to Litchfield Hills and Stonebridge Manor. I look at him and shake my head. "I knew you'd take his side. My husband's mistress is moving into the guesthouse. What do you expect me to do, Michael? Just ignore her?"

"This is the trouble with you, Jessie: you've always gotten everything you wanted and once something doesn't go your way you get aggressive." Michael waves a hand toward the road. "Driving like a maniac doesn't solve anything and it's in your best interest to do whatever John wants you to. As his wife, you're supposed to support him. How stupid do you figure it will make him look, if he needs to tell Rebecca she can't stay?" His lip curls into a sneer. "Everyone in the office will say he's under the thumb. That's not a very good look for an executive partner, is it? Each time he needs to go away for a meeting with a client you start complaining. How do you think that makes him feel? Then you start hanging out with an author you met five minutes ago—in public so everyone can see. Do you know how many people saw you in the bistro with him? Gossip like that can ruin people's careers—especially mine. The boss already knows what you're like. He doesn't want you at any client dinner parties. You've been holding John back for years and soon it will affect me as well. Leaving him will be the last straw. Turn this car around and go back and apologize."

I stare at him in disbelief. How could he say such a thing about me? Does he believe I'm having an affair with Alex too? "Stop yelling at me. What you're saying is lies. What I do can't possibly affect your standing in the company. I'm surprised you're still working and not off overseas living the life with the amount of money that Grandma left you. I know Mr. Collins has already distributed the funds to you and Mom. I'm the only one who hasn't received a cent yet."

"Yeah, that's right, you got everything." Michael shakes his head when I miss the turn and I take the next left, hoping to find my way back to the highway. "See, you don't know where you're going and you've driven this way a thousand times before. Stop the car at the next gas station and I'll get a cab home."

I accelerate. "Maybe you should get out here. I never imagined you were so greedy." I snort. "They say money changes people. Now I can see what you're really like."

"Slow down." Michael grabs the wheel and we wrestle with the steering. "No, don't bother. I have a solution to all our problems."

I stare at him. "What?"

He is so strong I can't turn the wheel. We fly along a straightaway but a sweeping bend at the end is coming up fast and I can't keep the car on the road. A small clump of trees on the corner is getting closer. I lash out at him, pummeling his arm. "Let go of the wheel. You'll kill us."

I try to stand on the brake but Michael's foot is on my side of the footwell. He's turning the wheel and screaming at me. My hands slip on the steering wheel as the headlights pick up a jack-o'-lantern hanging from the tree. Something hits my head and then the tree is right there. I'm screaming as metal screeches and glass shatters. In a cloud of white, the airbag explodes, hitting me in the face. Tree branches shatter the side window and impale me. Darkness creeps into my vision. I hear a door open and Michael's voice over the hissing of steam.

"Goodbye, Jessie."

THIRTY-FIVE

NOW

I'm screaming. Is it in my head? I'm opening my mouth but no sound is coming out. I can hear just fine, although I'm drifting into oblivion. I can't move my arms or legs—am I paralyzed? Have I suffered a stroke? I recall Michael's face as he talked about my girls. Why did he say things like that? My memories of them are clear. I think back to the day they were born and remember everyone who was in the room. Seeing John with one in each arm, dressed in hospital scrubs and grinning like a baboon. I recall laughing at the nurse who said John was the only father she'd met in the delivery suite who looked immaculate in hospital scrubs. So many memories: the day they first walked—they did that a few minutes apart. Their first words, and taking them to school.

Has my mind created a fantasy? It all feels so real. Was I pregnant in the car wreck? No, that's not possible. I'm in my thirties. I know this and I had the girls in my twenties. It has to be a lie but why would my brother, who I love and trust, be lying to me? It makes no sense. Unless I overheard I'd killed my babies before I fell into the coma, and during the last year under sedation I created a life that never existed? The voices grow louder. I can hear John speaking to Dolly.

"Why is she restrained?" John is close by and he grips my hand. "She's sedated. I want those removed at once."

"She attacked her brother and was uncontrollable." Dolly's voice comes from the other side of my bed. "I needed to sedate her to get her back to bed. Her brother carried her in here. You don't understand when they get violent, they need to be restrained." She sighs. "Maybe you need to place her in a psychiatric hospital, although I'd hate to think what would happen to your reputation if the media got hold of the story."

"No, that's out of the question." John squeezes my hand and I tap his hand with my finger. "I'll sit with her for a time."

Footsteps disappear and John leaves me for a few seconds. The door closes and he is back, his cologne washing over me as he brushes a kiss over my lips. I want to open my eyes and tell him what happened, but the lids are so heavy and my body feels as if it's sinking into the bed. His warm hand closes around mine again. I move my fingers.

"I don't know if you can hear me, Jessie, but everything is going to be fine." John sighs. "From what Michael told us, and after the doctor examined you, we believe you're having flashbacks. It's a type of PTSD. When you've been in a coma it can tip you over the edge. When this happens you can't tell the difference between the flashback and reality."

I never saw a doctor and I tap my finger fast; it's the only thing I can move. It gets an immediate reaction.

"Are you trying to talk to me, Jessie?" John holds my hand gently.

I tap again. willing him to take notice of me.

"Okay, tap once for yes and two for no." John pulls up a chair and sits beside me.

I tap once.

"Do you know what happened to you?"

I tap once.

"Was it a flashback?"

I tap twice.

"Was it something I did?"

I tap twice.

"Do you know where you are?" John clears his throat when I tap once. "Do you know who I am?"

I tap once.

"Do you know who caused this to happen?"

I tap once and try very hard to write the initial M on his palm.

"Something Michael said to you made you attack him?" John sighs when I tap once. "He said you went ballistic and threw things at him. I spoke to Maria and she said you were screaming. Do you remember attacking him?"

I tap twice.

"Okay. I know you're in there and we've having a conversation. I know I caused all this to happen and I've been a jerk but you need to trust me. Can you do that, Jessie?" John sounds so sad.

I want to open my eyes and tell him everything is okay but whatever drug they've given me is making me like a zombie. I tap once. Right now he is the only lifeline I have. I need to face the fact that Michael has betrayed me. He tried to push me over the line and into insanity. There can be only one reason—money—but how did he find out about the conditions of the will? It was kept a secret to protect me—not that I should need protection from my own brother. Tears wet my cheeks in an uncontrollable stream.

"Oh, don't cry, sweetheart. I won't allow them to hurt you." John unfastens the restraints and tears them from the bed. "They won't be able to tie you down again. I'll insist they stop drugging you too. I'll ask Maria to keep an eye on you while I'm away." He lowers his voice and leans closer. "I'll find another nurse. I don't like the way Dolly treats you." He takes my hand again. "I wish I knew what Michael said to you. I don't believe his story and you're in no fit state to attack anyone. Do you want me to stop him from visiting you?"

I tap once.

* * *

John has been by my bedside for hours. Maria comes by to bring him coffee and meals. He makes phone calls, some to his boss and others to find a nurse from the agency. As time goes by, the numbness in my limbs decreases and I open my eyes. For once in his life, my husband is slightly crumpled. His hair is sticking up from where he must have been raking his hands through it. His shirt is open, tie hanging to one side, and he looks desperate. I can't believe he cares about me and then Alex's words come into my mind. When the private detectives were following me, he said John must be jealous. So maybe he cared enough then but why did he go and spoil everything by bringing Ms. Lawson into our home? I can't get my mind around it. Do I trust him or not?

"Do you want a drink?" John uses the control to lift the bedhead and then holds a straw to my lips.

I drink but my head is swimming from just sitting up a little. I try to speak and my voice sounds foreign to me. I want to ask him about the girls so bad but what if Michael was telling the truth and I've lost my mind? I can't risk it, not yet. I'll start with something easier. "I didn't try to kill myself, John."

"I read the note, Jessie, but it doesn't matter, you're alive." He places the water on the bedside table. "I searched everywhere for you the night of the wreck."

I try to focus on him, my vision blurs and then comes back. "I wasn't contemplating suicide. I couldn't live with you and Ms. Lawson and decided to leave. I was coming here."

"There were no skid marks, Jessie. The cops said you aimed for the tree." John takes my hand again. "It's history, don't worry about it now."

I shake my head but it makes me dizzy. "I'd never kill myself. The car was out of control. I recall that much. I remember trying to steer it and the steering locked or something." I look him straight in the eye and tighten my grip on his hand. "Was I pregnant when I wrecked the SUV?"

"No... well, not that I'm aware." His Adam's apple bobs up and down. "The doctor at the E.R. never mentioned it. So no, I don't believe so. Why?"

Exhaustion grips me and I lie back. Asking him about the girls now would make me appear crazy if Michael was telling the truth. I look at him. "Do you believe me about the wreck?"

"Yeah. I couldn't believe it but Michael said you'd mentioned it before." He squeezes my hand. "If you ever feel that way again, tell me and I can get help for you."

My throat is raspy and it's difficult to talk. "He's lying. I've never contemplated suicide—leaving you, yes, many times especially in the early years of our marriage. You weren't a good husband to me, John, and you know it. The thing is I loved you and hoped you would change and then you wanted Ms. Lawson to move into the guesthouse and that was the last straw."

"I've been an ass. I took you for granted and I'm sorry." He shakes his head. "I'm glad you're starting to remember what happened. The good and the bad." He checks his watch. "It's almost three. I need to go home. I have a meeting first thing that I can't get out of and believe me I've tried."

Panic grips me. He can't possibly leave me alone with Dolly. "Stay here. You can drive home in the morning. Dolly might drug me again."

"She's asleep and won't be by to see you. I told her I'd stay." He pats my hand. "I'll have a new nurse here as soon as I can. I told Dolly no more drugs or restraints. Maria will tell me if she doesn't do as I say."

I don't want him to leave but whispers of conversations drift around in my head. I heard Dolly talking to him on the phone and why did Michael leave me the note to warn me not to trust anyone unless he cared? Was he telling the truth after all? Is this attention just a ploy by John to lure me into a false sense of security—or is he the only person I can trust? A face drifts into my mind. He's not the only person. There is one more who has absolutely no interest in getting their hands on my estate—Alex.

THIRTY-SIX

I'm scared and helpless. I suddenly understand how a mouse feels when it sees a cat. It's like I'm in a huge empty cave, with monsters waiting to pounce on me. The noises in the big house sound louder than usual. I hear footsteps and no one arrives at my door. I'm sure Dolly will stick me with another needle the moment she sees me awake, but sleep keeps dragging me under and with it comes vivid dreams. I recall having fever dreams as a child but they are nothing like this. The confrontation I had with John over Rebecca Lawson moving into the guesthouse is breaking my heart. In my dreams, she is smiling at me from behind his back and he is all over her like a rash.

I'm thrown back through time and suddenly I'm pregnant and sitting at a party where John is entertaining another woman. As they turn on the dance floor, I see the woman is Rebecca. I try to stand, needing to confront him about her but I can't seem to move. The dream moves on, and I'm like a ghost in the hospital the night Daphne had Renee. Seeing John with her in the birthing suite tears out my heart but, as I drift closer in my ethereal state, I see it's not Daphne but Rebecca. The walls of the hospital close in around me and swirl like a sea of muddy water trying to carry me away. I'm suddenly in a flood, swimming for my life. I wake panting, all alone, as dawn washes away the darkness.

I sit up, disoriented and hold my head, trying to make out what's real and what isn't. Suddenly, memories slide into place. The night of the argument unfolds like a flower bud in my head but this bloom isn't beautiful. The love I have for John turns to hate. The need to get away from an impossible situation becomes abundantly clear. He gave me no choice. Why have I remained with him all these years? I've been a fool but they say love makes people do crazy things. The night of the accident I'd planned to come here, to Grandma's house. It's always been a sanctuary until now.

Now I remember everything in vivid detail: The dash to the car the moment John disappeared with Ms. Lawson, and then Michael climbing in the car to stop me. He was the one who yelled at me. I can clearly see his hand on the wheel as I wrestle with the steering. I stare into the dim light. Michael, my loving brother, wants me dead. Somehow, he's discovered the conditions of the will and wants to make me appear as if I've lost my mind. It started with planting the seed that John was having an affair, and where he took Rebecca for lunch. He knew it would cause problems between us and then he told John I was having an affair and John had me followed. No wonder I had the constant feeling of being stalked. When that didn't send me crazy, he tried to kill me.

Has what he said about the girls been another lie? I must discover the truth before Dolly drugs me again, and this time overdoses me. She is in on this up to her eyes. Right now, I need to get away. I'll call Alex but the phone in the kitchen might as well be a mile away. I take in my situation. It seems Dolly planned for me to be in zombie mode for a long time by the wires and tubes attached to me. Removing the tubes is okay but the drip is difficult and I can't stop the bleeding. I rip out my hair tie and push it up my arm and over a wad of tissues to staunch the flow. Giddy, I sway in bed, and my legs turn to Jell-O as I lower them to the floor. I grip the handle of the walker and take deep breaths. I can do this.

I turn off the machines; they haven't made a sound, but what if there's an alarm in Dolly's room? If she comes running, I'm toast. I take a deep breath and move off. It's difficult for me to walk with so many drugs in my system. I'm afraid of being caught, and move slowly along the dark passageway toward the kitchen. As I go past Dolly's room, I hear her coughing, and freeze on the spot when a light shines from beneath her door. Panic grips me as floorboards creak and I stare at the doorknob, waiting for it to turn. I wait agonizing seconds for the light to turn off. My heart races as the second I move off again the wheels on my walker squeak. I stop again and my legs tremble with fear. If she finds me out here, she will easily overpower me. I'm weak and she will stick me with a needle so fast I wouldn't see it coming.

It's quiet at last and I move my heavy legs as fast as possible. Perspiration drips from my brow as I finally make it into the kitchen. I turn on the lights and glance at the notepad by the phone, sagging with relief at the sight of Alex's phone number. I make the call and wait forever until he picks up. "Alex, they're drugging me. I remember everything. I need to get away from this place before they kill me. Please will you come? I'll meet you in the conservatory."

"They're what?! Holy cow, Jessie." Alex's footsteps clatter on tile. *"I'll throw on some clothes and come right away."*

I hang up the phone and slowly make my way back to my room. The walk exhausts me but I must keep going. I grab a couple of spare pillows from the closet and arrange them on the bed, to make it look like I'm under the blankets. I have very few clothes and they all fit into the compartment under the seat of my walker. I've used every last ounce of strength, and dressing takes me forever. Sweat trickles down between my shoulder blades as I push the walker to the conservatory. I open the door to the garden and allow the cool breeze to wash over me as I listen for the sound of a vehicle.

Birdsong breaks the silence as the sun creeps above the horizon, sending a golden glow across the garden. The heavy scent of roses is thick on the breeze. This is a beautiful home and I'm sad to leave it, but once I'm in control of my inheritance, I'll hire people to protect me. It seems like a lifetime before Alex arrives. "Alex, I have so much to tell you. I know who was in the car with me the night I had the accident. It was Michael... he grabbed the steering wheel and aimed my car at the tree. He tried to kill me."

"We need to get out of here right away." He scoops me into his arms. "I'll come back for the walker. I want you safely in my truck. Lock all the doors until I get back."

Safe inside his truck, I watch as he runs back to collect my walker. The lights in the house come on, and panic grips me as I see Dolly yelling at him. She is grabbing at the walker but Alex wrestles it away and he's heading toward me at a run. He tosses the walker into the back of the truck as I lean over to unlock his door. "Are you okay?"

"I'm fine. I just hope she doesn't call the cops. Luckily, she doesn't know me so we should be fine." Alex starts the engine, and we roar off down the road at high speed. He flicks me a glance. "You look dreadful. How long has this been going on?"

I tell him about Michael and what he told me. "I'm too frightened to ask John if the twins exist or if I manufactured them during my coma as a way to cope with what had happened."

"I wish I could help you but I've never seen them, so if they are a figment of your imagination, I'm the wrong person to ask. I can say that you didn't look pregnant to me and you mentioned them *before* the accident. This means you didn't create them during the coma." Alex stares at the road ahead. "Who can you call that you trust implicitly?" He clears his throat. "Someone who won't benefit from you not inheriting the estate and someone who—if you are, as you say, manufacturing them—won't have you committed."

I can think of only two people, my mom and dad. "The only problem is I don't know where they are or their contact numbers. I had them on my phone and who remembers phone numbers anymore? I know mine and John's but that's all."

"We might be able to find them." Alex keeps driving. "Stay positive. You're doing fine and there's nothing wrong with your mind." He glances at me. "Were the girls in the SUV with you the night of the wreck?"

I nod. "I'm afraid so. I remember putting them in the car and making sure they fastened their seat belts. It was late and they fell asleep right away." I tap my heart. "In here I know they're real. I recall one of them calling out after the accident." I think for a beat and then turn in my seat to look at him. "Michael was in the vehicle; I know this for sure but he walked away and left the girls. I know at least one of them was conscious and the airbags would have deployed. One of them must have seen him. If they're alive, why didn't they see him and tell someone?"

"Do you recall what he was wearing?" Alex turned toward me.

I close my eyes and see him jumping into the passenger seat. The girls are asleep already. I open my eyes. "He's wearing a hoodie and the girls are asleep. If he jumped from the SUV on impact, they wouldn't have seen him. It was dark, he was wearing black and there was a lot of steam."

"I've seen the wreck." Alex stares straight ahead. "It was taken to the yard beside the police station. Only the front driver's side is damaged and the window. It doesn't make sense you having an injury to the right side of your head, and hard enough to fracture your skull."

The dream must have been a real memory and the implications shake me to the core. "I can't believe I'm saying this but it has to be Michael. I remember being hit in that side of the head just before the accident, not after. A pain shot through my temple just before I hit the tree. It made me bite my tongue and I tasted blood in my mouth." I point to my temple. "It was right here. It was real hard. I figured it was a dream but since then I've remembered the accident, right down to the jack-o'-lantern hanging from the tree I hit. That part of it was no dream."

"If your recollections are true, this is a matter for the cops." Alex stops in front of his garage and waits for the door to slide open. He drives inside and then turns to look at me. "Honestly, I couldn't write this stuff. It's not as if he was left out of the will. Most normal people could live comfortably on that amount for the rest of their lives. How much does he need?" He scratches his cheek. "Unless he has a gambling problem or something like that? Have you known him to gamble?"

I shake my head. "Not in any normal way, no, but investments are always a gamble."

"That's food for thought. Wait up and I'll get your walker and we'll go inside." He smiles at me. "On the subject of food, I'm starving, and I make a mean omelet. We'll talk about this in the kitchen while I'm cooking."

I sigh; the idea of being away from Dolly makes me light-headed. "That sounds like a plan."

THIRTY-SEVEN

After breakfast, Alex shows me around the house. It's neat and tidy, and the house is beautifully furnished, with comfy modern furniture. His taste runs to clean lines, glass-topped wooden tables, swirls of color spread across the rugs, but all the walls are white. The background is perfect for his pictures. The landscapes are like windows to another space. I look at him. "For a writer, your house is spotless. Many don't have the time to fight deadlines and clean house or the spare cash to pay for a cleaning service. I was lucky, I had a housekeeper to help me clean up after the girls. She did most of the cooking as well."

"I have a service, they do the house and the yard, although I created the backyard myself over a year or so." Alex indicates to my walker. "I assume your clothes are in here. Do you need help to hang them in the closet?"

"Yes, thanks." I open the seat of my walker and scoop up my underwear. "Are the drawers empty?"

"Yeah." He pulls one open for me. "There you go." His gaze locks with mine. "Will you be okay watching TV for a time? I have a deadline for some edits I need to finish."

I inhale the smell of cedar from the drawer; it's lined with clean paper with pine cones on it. I add my meager amount of underwear and then return his gaze. "I'd love to watch TV. I've been isolated for so long, breathing fresh air is a treat."

An hour or so later, I'm sitting on the sofa in the family room, watching TV, when the room fills with red and blue flashing lights. Someone is hammering on the front door and Alex comes out from his office where he's been working on his book to answer it. People are rushing in the room and a burly cop forces Alex onto his knees and cuffs him. John comes in behind them and stares at me. I'm trembling so much my teeth are chattering. "What's going on?"

"Did this man kidnap you?" A man wearing a suit with a badge on his belt, stands in front of me.

I shake my head. "No, he did not. I called him and asked him to come and get me because the nurse that was looking after me was drugging me. I have reason to believe my brother has been trying to kill me." I wave a hand toward Alex. "Leave him alone, he's only trying to help me."

The cops allow Alex to stand and he rubs his wrists.

I look at him. "I'm so sorry, Alex, I never meant for this to happen."

"It's okay." Alex's mouth twitches into a wry smile. "Someone needed to help you."

"What's all this about your brother trying to kill you?" The man in the suit is staring down at me again. "And while I'm here, I'd like to ask you some questions about your accident."

I lift my chin. "And you are?"

"Detective Jack Marshall. Your husband called us after your nurse found a telephone number and we traced it to Alex Harris. He mentioned he's an acquaintance of yours but has no idea why you'd call him. I was informed you had memory loss.

Obviously that problem has been resolved. I figure you need to tell me what's been going on."

I take my time and start from the beginning, leaving out the personal bits about John, me, and Ms. Lawson. "My husband had it in his head that I was involved with Alex and had me followed. Michael told me I had an overactive imagination but kept feeding me lies to keep me off balance. He intimated that John was having an affair with his company's lawyer. I believed it and when John asked her to move into our guesthouse, I decided to leave. Michael jumped into the car and we argued, he hit me in the temple and grabbed the steering wheel. He put me into that tree. I didn't try to kill myself or leave a suicide note. I was heading for my grandmother's home."

"One moment." The detective held up the hand with a pen in it to stop the conversation. "We know the SUV was new. Was Michael inside the vehicle before the night of the accident?"

I shake my head. "No, and he wasn't wearing gloves."

"Okay, it's in the police yard as the accident is still under investigation." The detective makes more notes. "I'll have it dusted for prints. Go on."

At last, proof that I'm telling the truth. I suck in a breath. "Weird things started happening in the house." I tell him everything in as much detail as I can recall. "The last straw was when Michael told me I'd been pregnant before the wreck and killed my twins. I was screaming at him when Dolly the nurse stuck me with a needle. I woke up unable to move and strapped to the bed."

"I visited her." John sits beside me on the sofa. "I was with her until three in the morning. I didn't discover she was missing until lunchtime. I was in a meeting."

"You left her there after all that's happened?" The detective raises both eyebrows.

"I didn't believe she was in any danger at the house." John

meets his gaze. "I gave the nurse instructions not to give her any medication and asked the housekeeper to keep an eye on her." He turns to look at me. "Why didn't you tell me everything? You didn't mention anything about him accusing you of killing our unborn children. You never mentioned you were pregnant before the car wreck."

Swallowing the lump in my throat, I look at him. *It's now or never. Am I crazy or am I sane?* "I wasn't. Michael tried to convince me that I'd imagined the girls, that I'd conjured them up during my coma. I didn't tell you because I wasn't sure if I was losing my mind." I turn to Detective Marshall. "I asked after them a thousand times but no one would tell me anything. I still don't know if they're dead or alive." I spin around and glare at John. "Now can you tell me the truth about my girls?"

"I told you not to worry about anything when you asked me. Dolly told me the doctor insisted I keep things general and not speak about family. We didn't know if you'd planned to kill yourself and the twins. It made you an unfit mother. You're not allowed to see them until we get this sorted. If I break the ruling, they'll be placed in foster care." John grips my hands and stares into my eyes; he looks stricken. "I believed I was doing the right thing, Jessie. It was tearing me up inside, seeing you so upset. You don't need to worry a moment longer. The girls are fine. They're with your mother. They were in Florida, as I couldn't look after them alone. Our housekeeper left the week after you wrecked the car." He sighs. "They've been here since you woke from the coma. Your mother took them straight to your grandmother's house and they gathered some flowers for you. Dolly sent them away. She knew you weren't allowed to see them. I can see now that Dolly and Michael are working together and I played right into their hands. Everything they've said is a lie. I'd like to know the reason they wanted to harm you. Do you know what's going on, Jessie?"

Relief rushes over me and I nod. "He wants my money but I'm not sure why as he inherited a ton from Grandma's will."

"I believe I do." Alex sat in a chair opposite and everyone turns to stare at him. "When Jessie believed someone was following her and Michael made a big deal out of it rather than doing something, I had my suspicions something was wrong. I'm not sure why but he was just acting strange. I had my portfolio with him and asked it to be moved to another person in the office. If he doesn't have a gambling problem, I would seriously suggest looking into his clients' accounts."

"Embezzlement?" John's eyebrows rise as he reaches for his phone. "I'll order an audit immediately." He walks into the kitchen.

"He wouldn't inherit your grandmother's estate if you died, would he?" Detective Marshall was making copious notes in a little book.

I explain. Telling him that Grandma didn't trust John as Michael had told her he was having an affair with Rebecca Lawson and I should rewrite my will and give the estate to Michael and not John if I died. I rest my gaze on him. "What doesn't make sense is how he discovered that I'd changed my will to leave everything to him. My lawyer would never disclose anything to him. He's been our lawyer for as long as I can remember. He even kept the conditions of my inheritance secret from the rest of the family. I was the only one in the room, when the documents were signed."

"I believe I'm going to need a little talk with your brother." Detective Marshall stands. He moves his attention from Alex to John. "I'm not going to need to come back here again, am I? Are you two cool?"

They both nod and the detective turns to me. "What about you? Are you returning home with your husband?"

I shrug. Too much has happened for me to just return home.

I need a long talk with John. "I haven't decided yet. I don't even know if he wants me to go home with him."

"Okay, I'll leave you to sort that out." Detective Marshall holds his pen above the notepad. "I need your brother's details. I'm gonna go and pay him a little visit. Is he at the office at this time of the day?"

"Yes, he is. You'll find him on the third floor." John gives him all the details he needs.

As the cops file out, Alex looks from one of us to the other.

"I'll get back to work and leave you two to talk. I figure you need to sort this out between you. However if you have a problem, Jessie, you're welcome to stay here for as long as you like. I have plenty of spare rooms." He looked at John. "There's nothing going on with us. Jessie is like my little sister. I don't intend to come between you."

I smile at him. "Thanks, Alex, you're a good friend to me." I turn to John. "Okay, I want to know everything."

THIRTY-EIGHT

"I know the first few years of our marriage were rough." John pushes a hand through his immaculate hair. "What happened at the party that night was a terrible mistake. I was an idiot and I should have known better but I've never been unfaithful to you, Jessie, never."

I roll my eyes, looking up to the ceiling for divine intervention and then I level my gaze on him. "That's not the entire truth, is it? Is Renee your child or not? How about we have the truth this time?"

"Yes, she's my child but it's not what you think. Daphne was desperate to have a baby and Brad was infertile. She asked me to be their donor and I agreed. I didn't know Brad would flip out and leave her."

I stare at him, astonished. "So you ran around to her house for breakfast with sex on the side?"

"No! I didn't have sex with Daphne. I was a sperm donor. We had an agreement. I made Daphne sign a legal document, to say that she would never pursue me for maintenance and my name wouldn't appear on the birth certificate. However, she did give me the honor of naming our daughter."

Dumbfounded, I look at him. I can't grasp what he's saying. All this time, all these years he's kept a secret. My girls have a sister they'll never know. I can't believe my ears. "A sperm donor? I guess you expect me to believe that? Did you go to a fertility clinic with her? Do you have proof?"

"You know darn well she was attending a fertility clinic and yes, you can come with me to speak to the doctor if you don't believe me." John wipes a hand down his face. "I knew you'd never understand, that's why we didn't tell you."

Suddenly it was "we" and I push down the need to get up and walk away from him. I swallow hard trying to control the anger ready to explode. "So it's 'we' is it? You conspired with my once-best friend to have a baby. No wonder Brad left her. I guess seeing you turning up for breakfast every morning would ruin most people's marriages." I draw in a breath. "Why you? Fertility clinics usually have a variety of sperm donors she could have used."

"She didn't want a stranger's baby and we were close friends. In truth, I felt sorry for her." He shrugs and opens his arms wide. "So I made a mistake. I can't change it now."

I shake my head. "Sorry for her? That's not an excuse for not discussing it with me first."

"Would you have agreed?" John clears his throat. "I'm guessing the answer is no."

I shake my head. "Then you'd be right. You're my husband and the father of my children. If I'd wanted to share, I'd have joined a wife-swapping club or whatever they call them. I'm appalled you'd even consider doing something like that behind my back. What else aren't you telling me?"

"I supported her after her marriage breakup and until a year after Renee was born. I was the father, after all, and wanted to make sure my child wants for nothing. I set up a trust fund so she can go to college." He stares at the space between his hands at the swirls on the carpet. "I figured that was the right thing to do."

I shut my open mouth with a snap. "A trust fund? Do the twins have one too?"

"Of course they do and it's five times bigger than Renee's." John frowns. "Hers is more than enough though to put her through college and then some."

This is a nightmare, it's like he has a whole separate life. Just like my dad. Seems to me Grandma smelled a rat about both of them. "Do you keep in touch with her?"

"Yeah, she sends me photographs and videos of Renee. I keep them in the office." John shrugs. "I realize now, I should have told you but I'm not sorry. She's a beautiful child."

I shake my head slowly. "It seems to me you have no faith in me whatsoever, if you couldn't trust me with something like that. All these years not knowing and believing you'd been unfaithful was much worse. It's caused a big rift between us. I've never trusted you since the night Renee was born and you left me alone to be at Daphne's side. Each time I think of it, it breaks my heart. I'm just glad I didn't have to go to my grave believing you were unfaithful. Although, going behind my back to keep in touch with her is another form of betrayal."

"You're so jealous, I was afraid to tell you the truth in case you left me. Now I can see how it's affected you, I realize I should have come clean years ago. Honestly, Daphne was our close friend, I wanted to help her is all. Maybe I should have discussed it with you. At the time it was just a good deed. I guess, I didn't think it through. I believed you'd be happy for her." He drops his head into his hands and stares at the carpet again. "Is there anything I can do to mend this between us?"

I can't believe my ears; he can't expect me to believe this crap. I wet my lips, my throat is parched and I reach for a glass of water on the coffee table. "So because I love you and I'm jealous of other women pawing you, that's your excuse for deceiving me? I asked you so many times about Renee and you lied to me. How can I possibly trust anything you say?"

"I don't know." He grips my hands. "Can we start over? If not for me for the sake of the girls?"

I refuse to be a doormat or a faithful dog any longer. "I can't forgive you for deceiving me yet, John. Hurt like that takes time to heal and I can't take any more lies. If you promise to be faithful and come clean about Rebecca Lawson I might think about it."

"How many times must I tell you? There's nothing between me and Rebecca." He lifts his gaze to me. "There never has been and there never will be. She's the company lawyer is all."

I frown at him. "Oh, come on, John, there are images of you with her all over her social media page. Pictures of you with her at swank dinner parties, and all the time I was sitting at home. How do you think that made me feel when I found them?"

"The dinner parties, as you call them, were corporate meetings in the board room with important overseas clients." John rubs the back of his neck. "It was all business talk and not a place for wives. Everyone there was employees of the company in important roles." He drops my hands and leans back in the chair. "Not that you'll ever believe me."

I snort. "Well, it's difficult when you bring her home to live in our guesthouse and from what Michael tells me she's still there. Well, she's inside the house now. Explain that?"

"She's never stayed inside the house, Jessie." John gives me an astonished stare. "I can't believe Michael told you that. It's all lies. She stayed over the night of the accident and then went to a hotel. FYI, she's getting married to her longtime boyfriend and they're moving to Hawaii." He sighs. "I'm interviewing her replacement now. The best candidate for the job this time is someone called Jason Standish. Somehow, I don't believe you'll have a problem with me having lunch with him."

Knowing Ms. Lawson would be out of our lives makes me

feel more positive about things but he did still switch off my life support. I look at him. "Do you love me?"

"You know I do." John's eyes soften. "That will never change."

I think it through. What do I need to make it right? "I'm not going back to Grandma's house. Not until I'm strong. I'm not going home—not yet anyway. I want time to figure out how I feel about everything. I want to see my girls and talk to my mom and dad. In the meantime, Alex has told me I can stay here."

"No, I don't want you staying here." John shakes his head. "You hardly know him and you're moving in with him. It's not a good look, Jessie."

I puff out a sigh. "Neither is having a secret family on the side, John. How long before you decide to leave me and go and live with Daphne?"

"I would have done it by now, wouldn't I?" John rolls his eyes. "She is just a friend. I've never found her attractive in that way."

I nod. "That's the same with me and Alex."

"Okay, okay, I get your point." He shakes his head. "I'll go home and ask your mom to drop by to see you before the girls finish school. She's been caring for them at home since you regained consciousness. Are you sure you don't want me to take you there now? She'll be so happy to see you."

As tempting as it is, I have too many things to consider. I need to think this through. The cops will arrest Michael and I need to tell my mom everything that happened. She'll tell me what to do. I shake my head. "Not today. I need time to think, John. Is my dad there too?"

"Nope, he's in Florida." John pulls a phone from his pocket and hands it to me. "This is for you. I had intended on giving it to you when I went to see you. I've added all your contacts so you can speak to him." He checks his watch. "If you're not coming home with me, I'll need to go to work. I'll move my appointments around so I can come back and see you later." He stands and bends to kiss me. "If you want to see me?"

I look into his deep blue eyes. I so want to trust him again. "That would be nice, thank you."

I watch as he leaves, closing the door behind him and then turn as Alex walks back into the room.

"How did it go?" Alex drops into the chair opposite. "I did catch bits of conversation but I tried not to listen."

I sigh. "I figure it's a work in progress. At least the girls are real and I'll get to see them soon."

"I never had any doubt." He grins, showing an expanse of white teeth. "I have a feeling everything will turn out just fine."

THIRTY-NINE

The next morning, I walk along the path in Alex's garden to see his fishpond. He has the Japanese theme going on and it's like stepping into another world. Against a serene backdrop of vibrant greenery in lush green hues a small bubbling fountain spills water into a crystal-clear fishpond. I follow a carefully maintained path winding its way through the foliage and find a graceful wooden bridge arching over the fishpond. I immediately relax. I have the sun on my face and the breeze in my hair. "This is beautiful. Did you create this yourself?"

"Yeah, it took me a long time but it was food for my imagination." Alex chuckles. "You would be surprised how many books I've written in my head out here." His hand comes under my elbow. "Are you strong enough to walk over the bridge and look at the fish?"

I inhale the fresh air and smile at him. "If we take it slow, I'll be fine."

As I walk across, I pause to gaze down at the shimmering water and see koi of various colors—orange, white, and gold—sliding gracefully beneath the surface, some stopping occasionally, their mouths open to catch dragonflies. I can see the entire garden from my perch. Alex has created a work of art. Tall bamboo stalks sway gently in the breeze and stone lanterns, as if weathered by time, stand like sentries along the pathway and cast soft dappled shadows in the sunlight. I can see his hand in the creation; it's so like his landscapes. It's a peaceful retreat from the outside world. "So this is the view from your office. It's wonderful. Are those cherry blossom trees? They must smell wonderful in spring."

"They do." A loud hammering comes from inside. "What the hell—?"

I move slowly down the slope of the bridge. "Go and see who it is. I'll be fine."

As Alex heads into the house, the banging gets louder. A scuffle comes from inside and then male voices shouting. The next moment, Michael bursts through the glass doors to the garden, his face red and furious. Behind him, Alex is trying to slow his progress by grabbing him by the arm. Fear grips me; as I step from the bridge, my knees tremble as Michael drags Alex toward me. "What do you want, Michael?"

"You set the cops on me, didn't you?" Michael gets up close in my face. "You're crazy. Trust me, if I wanted to kill you, you'd be dead already." He glares at me. "The cops came to my office—my office, Jessie. How do you figure that looks to my clients? I needed to make up an excuse about someone breaking into my house. Now, I've been suspended from work and the cops are monitoring my phone calls. They insisted I surrender my passport or they were going to arrest me." He points at me. "You did this. I wish you'd died in the wreck. You've ruined my life." He shrugs Alex's hand from his arm and turns to him. "She's batshit crazy. You wouldn't believe all the lies she told me. Like she'd killed her unborn baby and she hears phones ringing in the night when they're disconnected." He takes a step back and his mouth turns down. "She told the cops I was in her car when she wrecked it, that I forced her into the damn tree. I wanted her dead so I could get her inheritance." He shook his head. "They have no evidence because there isn't any."

I keep the walker between us. "How did you know that I changed my will?"

"I spoke to Mr. Collins the day he read the will. He asked me to get you so you could sign the codicil. I was right outside, Jessie. I heard everything. Nice of you to think of me. I figured everything would go to John if you died." He chuckles.

I see red. "That's the reason you want me dead."

"I have money." Michael shakes his head. "I don't need to kill my sister for it. You need help."

I see a flicker of doubt in Alex's eyes and my stomach drops. "I know what you did, Michael. You turned Grandma against John and Dad, telling lies about them. After I read Grandma's letter you convinced me that John was having an affair. That was the start of trying to make me look like I was going mad."

I need to know the truth about one more thing. When Michael's angry he forgets secrets, so I allow the lie to slip through my lips. "I know you convinced John to switch off life support. How could you?!"

"I knew he'd tell you." Michael shook his head. "We didn't want you to suffer."

I poke him in the chest. "Bullshit! You wanted me dead. You made Dolly keep me in a drug-induced coma and when I came out of it you tried to make me look as if I'd lost my mind. You started by sending me a note, telling me not to trust anyone."

"See." He waves a hand toward me. "Crazy." He looks at Alex. "She was becoming unbalanced long before the accident. She believed people were following her and then she tried to kill herself. She left a note, Alex. Whatever she's told you about me is a lie."

I can't believe my ears. "I don't know why the cops let you

go but I'll prove everything and, by the way, I'm changing my will. If anything happens to me, you'll get nothing."

"Ha. You can't change your will unless you're of sound mind, sweetheart," Michael sneers at me as he heads for the door. "You're crazy and I'll make sure everyone knows. They'll never let you have your kids. You tried to kill them in the wreck. You're unfit to be a mother."

I slump against the bridge and tears stream down my cheeks. I can't fight him any longer. I look at Alex as he observes me from under his lashes. "I'm not crazy. I'm not."

FORTY

THREE DAYS LATER

I'm staying with Alex and I still haven't seen my kids. Michael moved swiftly and viciously to contact child protection to inform them that I'm still unstable and need to be kept away from my girls. He insisted he'd read the suicide note and gave a damning statement. So now they want a report from a psychiatrist and I'll need a court order if I'm ever to see them again. John has been to see me a number of times and informs me that he destroyed the so-called suicide note.

Surprisingly, he has been very supportive and informed them that Michael was lying and the note said only I was going to my grandmother's house and that there wasn't a threat of suicide in it. I guess I owe him big time for that because there was no intent on my part. He did tell them that I left after we'd had a disagreement but as I didn't drive away in an erratic manner, he had no cause for concern. He also informed them that it was taking time for me to regain my memory after the accident and the children were safe in his custody and being cared for by my mother. The interview I had with the child protection officers was tense.

"You must understand, Mrs. Harper, that we take every complaint seriously and act swiftly to protect the children." The woman wearing a fitted white and gray pencil skirt with loafers peers at me over the top of her glasses. Her friend remains silent staring at me as if I'm a serial killer. "The fact it was your own brother who upgraded the complaint adds another layer of concern."

I remain calm, and having Alex close by listening to the conversation as my witness makes me feel a whole lot better. "I have nothing to hide but I'm sure that Michael didn't tell you that he was in the vehicle with me when it was wrecked." I look from one to the other and see their blank expressions; it's like talking to brick walls. "He grabbed the steering wheel and caused me to hit the tree. He then left the scene of the accident, leaving me and my girls alone in the car. We didn't get any help for two hours or more. If they had been injured, they could have died in that time. You know I've been in a coma for almost twelve months and it's taken me a little time to recall everything that happened."

"There is nothing in the police report about someone else being inside the vehicle." White Shirt narrows her gaze at me making me feel as if I'm in the Spanish Inquisition.

I take in the lines around her mouth, and the way she puckers her lips in distaste as she observes my every move. It's as if she has already made up her mind. "The police only spoke to me a couple of days ago and I explained that Michael was in the car. He wasn't wearing gloves so his fingerprints will be all over it. It's a new SUV and to my knowledge he'd never been inside it before that night. The detective who interviewed me said he'll dust it for prints. It will prove I'm telling the truth."

"Very well." White Shirt stands and pushes a notepad into her briefcase. "We'll review your case once we've heard from the police. In the meantime, the restrictions on visiting your children are still active." She narrows her gaze on me. "If you break the rules, Mrs. Harper, the twins will be placed in foster care." She heads for the door and her companion follows close behind. "There's no need to see us out."

I turn to Alex and shrug. "They're a law unto themselves, aren't they? I don't believe they listened to a word I said."

"I know I shouldn't get involved, Jessie, but I really believe you should have a lawyer present when you speak to them next time." Alex sat on the arm of the sofa, one leg swinging. "The last comment she made came close to a threat. I'm sure you can go to court to have this ruling reversed."

I nod. "I'll speak to John. He'll know what to do."

The doorbell chimes and Alex heads to see who's there. A few seconds later he returns to the family room and raises both eyebrows at me. Concerned, I stand behind him but I can't see who's waiting outside. "What's wrong?"

"Nothing's wrong." Alex indicates over one shoulder with his thumb. "It's your dad. I know you two weren't seeing eye to eye prior to the accident so I figured I should ask you before I allowed him to come in."

It's true. The relationship between me and my dad had never been the same since we discussed the second family he supported. I'd been sad that he hadn't come and seen me. My mother had been by and shown me videos of the girls she'd taken before school. I'd told her everything and she assured me that I should put things behind me and move forward which I intend to do. When I'd mentioned my dad, she shook her head. He didn't want to see me. I'd never discussed the other family with her as I'm still unsure how much she knows.

I nod. "Sure, we need to mend bridges."

My father looks tanned and healthy; the reduction in work and living in Florida obviously suits him. I smile as he walks toward me. "Hi Dad. I'm really glad you're here."

"Me too." He hugs me. "I'm so sorry I put you through all this. I couldn't forgive myself when you had the accident. I figured we'd lost you. When your mom told me you had recovered, I couldn't wait to see you."

I lead him to the sofa and sit down. "It's been tough since I woke from the coma."

"I hear that Michael is giving you a hard time." He sits beside me on the sofa. "I've been concerned about him for a long time. He came to me a month before your grandmother died, asking for a loan. It was substantial and I couldn't get it out of him what he wanted it for. I told him if he needed that amount of money, he needed to go through the bank. Now John tells me that the audit on his clients' books isn't looking good."

I stare at him uncomprehending. "What does this mean?"

"Simply, your brother's a crook, and a liar, and I've been covering his ass for years." He shakes his head in obvious despair. "Well, I should have told your mother about Andrea Long and her daughter Michelle but then I would have needed to explain and, in your mother's eyes, Michael can do no wrong. The truth is, Andrea was underage when she became pregnant. She was living with her grandmother months into the pregnancy and then her grandmother passed, leaving Andrea homeless. She has no other living relatives and when she went to Michael, he denied absolutely that it was his child. She hunted me down and her story made a lot of sense to me. The timing of where she met him, and the fact she knows about the birthmark on his right hip, made me, let's say, more than a little suspicious."

I feel that if my eyes get any wider they'll fall out and roll across the floor. I can't believe my ears. "I figured that Michael preferred older women."

"He does now." Dad rolls his eyes. "When Andrea told me she was going to the cops, I needed to do something. I couldn't tell your mom; she is a valued member of the community and a scandal like that, in this close environment would have ruined her."

I wave a hand at him. "Anyway, so Michael was in trouble and you decided to bail him out?"

"Yes, I contacted Andrea again and set her up in an apartment. I supported her until she had the baby and then we conducted a DNA test. I used my own DNA for a comparison and, being Michael's father, it came back as a grand paternal match. Michelle is my granddaughter, although Michael still denies he even met Andrea." He meets my gaze. "I feel obliged to support Andrea. Now, since she finished college and has a job, it's not the same. I help out when necessary, like any grandparent, and I set up a trust fund for college for Michelle."

I can't believe my ears. "What else has Michael lied about?"

"Too many things to list." Dad sets his weary eyes on me. "I must tell your mom. I know Michael has a gambling problem. It was only a matter of time before he started embezzling from the firm. If he has, I won't be able to buy him out of trouble again."

I blink, trying to make sense of it all. "He just inherited a lot of money; he can't be broke."

"I'm not sure, but from what John told me about the audit, he's been running some type of Ponzi scam, where he takes money from investors and pays them with other investors' money. It's doomed to fail because if one person wants to cash in, it causes a problem. He had four clients cash in this year. He needed to pay them or he'd be caught. He negotiates million dollar deals daily... well, he did. He's suspended right now." He holds my hand, linking our fingers. "I figure he knew about the will and was so desperate for money, he tried to kill you. He borrowed money from some shady characters and they don't like not being paid on time. I'd say they threatened him and might just do that if he doesn't pay them."

Sorrow engulfs me. "Why didn't he tell me the truth? Once the estate came into my hands, I'd have helped him."

"There is no helping him, Jessie." Dad shook his head, his face suddenly older. "Trust me, I've tried. He'd have taken every cent you own. John will call the cops if the books prove he embezzled from the company. He'll go away for a long time."

FORTY-ONE

It's the end of summer when the leaves start to turn golden and roses rush to spread their final blooms to the sun before fall arrives. The heavy perfume wafting from surrounding gardens invigorates me as I take my first steps into the garden unaided. The physical therapist who's been coming daily has helped me immensely but I'm still waiting to see my girls. Although we've been talking on FaceTime, it's not the same as hugging them and smelling their freshly washed hair. My mom comes by to see me often. She's caring for my girls and explained the difficulties in getting child protection to give me access. My case needs to go before a magistrate, so it might take a little longer.

Alex has been amazingly patient, I'm sure he didn't expect to have me as a visitor for so long. It's Sunday and John will be arriving soon. We have things to talk about. I've been bouncing a few ideas off Alex. The amount of research he does for his books gives him a good insight into crime and the way criminals think.

I can understand why John is a little hesitant toward me. In my mind I've been away from him for a few weeks but to him it's been over a year. I'm practically a stranger to him all over again. When he comes to visit me it's like being on a date and we're taking baby steps toward reigniting our relationship. I'm glad we're taking it slowly because, although I've never stopped loving him, trust needs to be earned. My stomach fills with butterflies when I hear a knock on the door. I push to my feet and he walks into the room and embraces me tenderly. I look at his immaculate blue shirt and gray chinos, so unusually casual I have the urge to ruffle his hair. He smiles as he pulls two crumpled pieces of paper from his pocket and hands them to me. "What's this?"

"Open them." He grins and his eyes twinkle. "The girls painted you pictures."

I hold them to my heart, feeling the tears spilling down my cheeks. "Oh, that's wonderful, thank you."

I open them and both of them are pictures of us as a family, all holding hands and in one is a little dog. "You have a dog?"

"Nope." John peers at the brightly painted pictures. "It's just wishful thinking on their part."

I laugh and suddenly we're a family again, with a bright future. I remember why I asked John to come around this morning. There are a few things we need to talk about. "Come into the kitchen. Alex has just put on a pot of coffee. I want an update on what's been happening."

"Okay, I'll tell you what I know but before I start, one question." John takes my hand and looks into my eyes. "When do you plan to come home?"

I get that squishy feeling in my stomach again. My heart races and I fall into his eyes. I want so much to go home with him. "The moment child protection tells me I can see my kids. I spoke to them on Friday and they said the case is still pending. They actually have no reason not to believe Michael." I head for the kitchen, still holding his hand.

We sit around the kitchen table, hot coffee steaming before us. I look at John. "I was talking to Alex earlier about how we can get around the problems I'm having with child protection. It all comes down to what happened after I woke from the coma. The police will establish that Michael was involved in the wreck when they discover his fingerprints but I figure it goes much further than that. I have no doubt in my mind that Michael was conspiring with Dolly to make me appear insane. Too many weird things happened when I woke up. Trust me, I was having trouble deciding what was real and what wasn't. Some of the things have already been explained, for instance, Mom told me you'd taken the girls' photographs and they are on our mantle."

"Yeah, we'd discussed that the day the will was read." John nodded. "Your mom wanted the others. What else happened?"

There's so much to tell him. "I saw Mom and the girls in the garden. Dolly lied to me and told me there was nobody there. Mom explained that she went with the girls to pick roses and Dolly told her I wasn't in any fit state to see her."

"That was a cruel thing to do." John shakes his head. "Tell me everything you remember."

Recalling the fear and disorientation I suffered seeing the fragrant blooms on my bedside table, I pause a beat to slow my heart rate. "Heaps of things, you see, Mom left the roses with the gardener and he took them inside the house and apparently put them into a vase. Maria found them there when she arrived and took them to my room. When I came out of the shower and saw them, I figured they must be a hallucination, the same as the girls."

"This means that Dolly was involved all the way along." Alex takes sips from his cup. "She has no end game. There's no obvious benefit for her in harming Jessie, so she must be working with Michael. He could have promised her a huge amount of money for her assistance." He rubs the back of his neck. "Think about it. She had access to all the drugs she needed to twist Jessie's mind. We know she was heavily sedated when she left the hospital." He looks at John. "You mentioned the reason for the medication to continue was to prevent her from having seizures—right? I bet that's a lie. What I'd like to know is, how did you come to pick Dolly for the job?"

"The nurse I had caring for Jessie wanted to work somewhere else, and I needed a replacement." John rubs his chin and stares into space for a few moments. "I recall asking Michael if he could look into a replacement. He came up with Dolly's name; in fact, he took it upon himself to interview her and gave her the job."

"Do you have the contact number of the previous nurse?" Alex glances at me and smiles. "Maybe it's time to give her a call and ask her why she really left?"

"Okay." John reaches inside his pocket for his phone, scrolls through the contacts and places the call. After introducing himself, and asking the question, the nurse's attitude changes.

"The patient's brother told me I wasn't maintaining her care and he'd report me if I didn't hand in my notice. It was a lie. I'm experienced with coma patients. The next thing I know, I run into Dolly at the agency, telling everyone her boyfriend has gotten her a peach of a job at a manor house. I chatted with her and discovered she was dating Michael Thompson."

Anxiety grabs me by the throat. I can't believe it! Dolly is Michael's girlfriend! I tremble with shock. The woman I trusted was working with him all the time and played a hand in trying to send me crazy. I grip the edge of the table so hard my knuckles go white. I look at John and his eyes flash with anger.

"Why didn't you contact me?" John flicks me a glance. "I hired you."

"From what Mr. Thompson told me, he was acting on your behalf."

"Well, he wasn't." John frowns. "I was very satisfied with your care of my wife and if you ever need a reference please call me." He disconnects and looks at me. "The plot thickens."

I look from one to the other. "Everything that happened, all the times I believed I was losing my mind, it was engineered by Dolly. She did everything in her power to turn me into a zombie."

"What's their motive? It must be one heck of a scheme to go to these lengths." Alex stands to refill the cups. "If we plan to lay out all this to the cops, we'll need to look at it through Michael's eyes."

Trying to get my head around the implications of the bombshell, I look at John, trying to remember the conversation I had with Dad. "It's all about money and getting Grandma's estate. I believe Michael is in serious financial trouble. When I spoke to Dad, he suggested a Ponzi scheme and possibly embezzlement from the firm. If Michael borrowed money from the wrong people, it might be a motive strong enough to kill me or try to prove I'm crazy."

"I hope you've acted on this hunch?" Alex looks at John.

"I have indeed but a full audit takes time and I've engaged experts to hunt down any schemes." John adds cream and sugar to his cup. "Friday's report was damning. I've updated the cops and they have Michael under surveillance. He's not going anywhere."

I turn my cup around with the tips of my fingers watching the rich brew swirl. "What about Dolly?"

"As far as I'm aware, she's still at the house and totally oblivious that we're on to her. My last conversation with her was that I intended to take Jessie back to the manor." John waves a hand dismissively. "You're aware the firm suspended Michael, pending an audit, and he still believes he can buy his way out of trouble? I've been very careful not to mention Dolly, so I imagine they still believe they can twist Jessie's mind enough for him to inherit under the terms of the will." John shrugs. "I haven't fired Dolly. I've had no reason to go back there since Jessie arrived here."

I think for a beat. "Mr. Collins will know if Dolly is still there. I'll call him in the morning."

"Don't bother, I'm paying for the upkeep and I employed Dolly and Maria." John smiles at me. "He fired everyone and I re-employed the ones I could find. I didn't want the house to fall into ruin. I admit if you'd died, I'd have turned it into a luxury hotel. That's what my mom and the Realtor were doing there when you came out of the coma. It was a feasibility study. A way of making the estate pay for itself and keeping it in the family."

I blink. "You're paying for the upkeep?"

"Yes." John squeezes my hand. "I know it's what you'd have wanted. That's why I took you to your grandmother's house and placed you near the rose garden. It's your favorite place. I figured if there was any chance of you waking up, it would be there. It worked, didn't it? Worst case, if you'd died, it would be in a beautiful place and not a sterile hospital room."

I allow the tears to fall. Not of sadness but happiness. All this time, I've pushed John away, and he was caring for me when I couldn't care for myself. "Oh, John. I've treated you horribly. I'm so sorry."

"Do you want me to give you some time alone?" Alex looks from John and back to me.

I shake my head. "Thanks, Alex, but we'll be fine." I turn to John. "I know now that Michael tried to turn me against you, feeding me lies. He made me believe you wanted me dead so you could control the estate. I was convinced that was the reason you asked me to sign the power of attorney."

"Oh, Jessie, I'd never want you dead. I found your grandmother's letter with her diary on the bedside table." John gives me a meaningful stare. "I read it just in case it had anything to do with your state of mind before the accident. I smelled a rat. I was trying to protect your inheritance from Michael. I just knew he was up to no good. Your dad tipped me off. He insisted that Michael had a hand in getting your grandmother to fire him —and he used that word too. He promised not to tell your mom and made up the need to retire."

Everything is suddenly making sense. "We need to have this out with Dolly. I want to know what doctor was supposed to be treating me. Nobody came to examine me when I woke, and she told me she was speaking to a doctor daily. I figure she's lying. I don't believe there was a doctor. All this crap about keeping me isolated to protect my sanity was the opposite. They were trying to make me believe I was losing my mind."

"Then we go and see her." John nods as if making up his mind. "We'll record everything she says and check all the equipment. The history on her computer will tell us if she's actually been contacting a doctor."

I hold John's gaze. "Did you speak to my doctor? Do you even know his name?"

"Of course, I spoke to the one at the hospital, he arranged everything with the nurse I employed to care for you." John rubs the back of his neck clearly agitated. "Dolly informed me the hospital doctor referred her to another doctor. I never spoke to him. I had no reason to. Dolly was giving me constant updates. In fact, she gave me more information than the other nurses I'd hired. I figured she was doing her job. If I'd known, I'd have fired her."

Memories of the torment I went through that first week shiver through me like ghosts. A thought hits me. "Why do you figure they decided to wake me?"

"I've been thinking about this too." John's brow crinkles. "If you weren't under a doctor for three months, perhaps the drug supply was running out. She had no choice. My guess is that she told Michael and they revised their plan."

"One thing." Alex looks at me his face set in stone. "Maybe you need to go back as a patient? She'll believe everything is okay. I doubt that Michael has contacted her. He wouldn't dare call her to discuss you over the phone, he knows his calls are being monitored." He frowns. "Although he might have dropped by to see her?"

"No, he hasn't. I instructed Maria to call me if anyone showed at the house." John met my gaze. "It will mean leaving you alone with Dolly while I check her computer. You'll need to keep her occupied."

Although my stomach clenches at the idea of returning to the house, I nod. "I can do that."

"It will be password protected." Alex frowns.

"Maybe but it doesn't matter." John smiles and wiggles a finger. "When I purchased it, I added both my facial recognition and fingerprint. I doubt she's smart enough to delete anything. I had a computer guy install everything a nurse would need to monitor you. It was set up before she arrived. She had no reason to change any settings."

I stand. "Okay, let's go."

FORTY-TWO

As I climb into John's Lexus, I notice one of the girls has left their pink sweater on the back seat. I grab it and press it to my nose. I'm sure a mom can find their child by scent. It might only be the smell from the laundry or the shampoo they use for their hair, but it triggers a response, a knowledge of belonging. Overwhelmed by the yearning to see my girls, I burst into tears. Nothing matters right now than seeing they're safe and well. The next moment John has his arms around me, my face pressing into his shoulder, and the scent unique to my husband fills my nostrils. It calms me and I gather myself, grasping the sweater like a life preserver. "I'm okay. I just miss my girls so much."

"We all miss you too." John started the engine and slid on his sunglasses. "It hasn't been easy for them being away from us for almost a year. Your mom is a wonderful person but she's not you and I could only get to see them a few times. They're so excited to be home and can't stop talking about you. They love the FaceTime chats." He squeezes my fingers. "It won't be long. I have my lawyer working on your case and I believe you'll be home soon."

I pull a tissue from a packet in the glovebox and dab at my eyes. "Not Ms. Lawson?"

"No, I engaged one that deals in family law. Her name is Julia Thompson and she'll represent you. I'm told she's very good." John flicks me a glance. "We'll go and see her on Monday."

I'm not sure I'm hearing him right. John never takes personal days. "You're taking me? What about your clients?"

"I rearranged my schedule." His hands grip the wheel as he stares straight ahead. "Now I'm a partner, I'll have more time to spare. I've spoken to the boss, and he agrees I need to spend some time with you. In fact, he suggested it. I've signed up some very important clients for the firm, which makes me valuable. I'll be home every weekend and I won't be working such long hours. I have many people working in my office who are more than happy for the opportunity to take on some of my clients."

Imagining my future unfolding, I lean back in my seat. "That would be wonderful."

As we fly along the coast highway, I open the window to absorb the view. The sight feeds my soul, as waves break on the beach, rush in and withdraw. They appear to shimmer as sunlight turns them into a mercuric firmament that leaves a line of foamy bubbles along the stretch of sand. I look into the distance, seeing sailboats, and sigh at the endless blue sky. I'm like a starving person at a smorgasbord. All the little things are magnified: seagulls strutting along the wet sand, fighting over a morsel of fish, and children running with joy as they splash through the waves. I want to join them with my girls and leave footprints in the sand. I can almost feel the salty brine on my face as waves crash around me. I lean my head out of the window, loving the wind in my hair. The roar of the ocean fills my head with a symphony of sounds. It's a peace I crave for and now it's within reach. Only a few more days and I'll be going home.

John and Alex are talking. It seems that John has accepted the fact that Alex is a friend and they are plotting how to get to Dolly's computer. I straighten in my seat, listening. "I don't believe you should allow Dolly to see both of you."

"How so?" John turns to look at me as we wait at the lights.

I stare back at him as the plan opens in my mind. "If Alex takes me back, he can keep Dolly busy and then pretend to leave by the conservatory." I turn to look at Alex in the back seat. "I'll keep her busy, when you leave. You'll need to set up your phone on record. If she tries to stick me with a needle, I want it on video."

"I'll go in through the front door and straight into her office." John drums his fingers on the steering wheel. "I'll download her patient records onto a thumb drive and look at her emails. I want to know who she's been calling for advice." He accelerates as the lights changed to green. "I should never have trusted her. I honestly believed you had the same doctor all the way through. How many times has a doctor visited you?"

I shake my head. "I don't recall seeing a doctor at any time."

"That's not good." Alex whistles. "It never amazes me what lengths people will go to for money."

The entrance to Stonebridge Manor comes into view. Ornate wrought-iron gates set between red-brick posts with lion's head statues greet us in an impenetrable barrier. We slow to allow the control on the dash of John's Lexus to trigger the opening mechanism as he drives toward them. They slowly swing open and he heads up the wide gravel driveway but doesn't go to the house. He takes the side road that leads to the rose garden and pulls up outside the gardener's shed. From here it's a short walk to the conservatory door.

"Ready?" John looks from me to Alex. "Give me time to scoot around the front. I have my key. I'll sneak in and head toward Dolly's office. I'll need as much time as you can get me."

I look at John. "Do you know if it's illegal to steal things from somebody's computer?"

"Legally the computer belongs to me, and I have a password." John shrugs. "So I doubt it." He slips from behind the wheel, shutting the door softly behind him, and jogs around the outside of the house.

Reluctantly, I leave the pink sweater on the seat as I climb out. I take Alex's arm and we head slowly toward the door to the conservatory. I look at him. "What are you going to say to her? What excuse are you making for bringing me back?"

"Oh, don't worry." Alex taps his temple. "I have a ton of stories in here. I'll make up something on the fly." As we reach the door, he cups his hands and looks through the window. "All clear."

I hold my breath as he slowly turns the doorknob. Trying not to make a sound, I follow him inside and we sneak through the pots of flowers. We pause at the door, standing on each side like cops in the movies, and peer into the room overlooking the rose garden. The scent of roses drifts through the open windows but the hospital bed is made, crisp and clean. The drip stand is placed close to the bed. My stomach drops. Nothing has changed. Everything is still the same as if waiting for my return... my slow death. Panic grips me. I can't do this. I dig my feet in, unable to move. I see Alex staring at me and I shake my head. Terror at Dolly administering the zombie drug again makes it hard to breathe. I pull back and sag against the wall, trying to force air into my lungs. Just being here is suffocating. I'm trusting Alex with my life. Have I just made a huge mistake? Just how well do I know him? What if he's part of the plan to get rid of me?

"Are you okay?" Alex turns to look at me, concern etched on his face. "I'll be close by. I won't allow her to do anything to you."

How can I explain? He hasn't been trapped here and under

her control. She's a monster and I'm still weak and vulnerable. She'll kill me for sure the first chance she gets. I grip his arm. "I can't do this. I'm terrified. She'll know something is wrong."

"Take deep breaths." Alex's voice is so low I can hardly hear it over the thumping in my ears. "Nothing will happen. I'll hide in here and watch her. It's the only way we'll be able to discover the truth. We need to stop her and Michael from ever trying this again."

Trembling, I consider his words and nod slowly. He's right, of course. I need my revenge and this is the only way of getting it. "Please don't leave me alone with her. She can't be trusted. I'm in fear of my life."

"I'll be right here in the shadows." He takes out his phone and wedges it between two figurines on a shelf and hits record. "It will record everything around the bed."

His assurances don't help. He hasn't experienced the feeling of being trapped inside his body like I have. I bite down on the inside of my mouth. I must do this for the girls. My legs tremble and my heart is racing so fast I'm sure it will burst through my ribcage. To think this house, once overflowing with love and memories of my family, has now changed into a torture chamber. *My torture chamber*. A mind-twisting place that altered my reality into a lie. I swallow the bile creeping into my mouth; the acid burns my throat and the bottled water beside the bed suddenly looks inviting. It's as if the bed is luring me as if I'm craving the drugs. I stop, my steps faltering. Dolly is inside my head, dragging me down a dark black hole. My mouth is dry and now my legs refuse to move. I don't want to go back. I can't do this—I won't. Blind panic grips me and I turn away. A cold sweat creeps over me and my T-shirt clings to my back. I can smell my own fear. I shake my head. "I can't do it. Something bad will happen. I can feel it."

"It won't." Alex turns me to face him. "I'll be here, six feet away, and John is just along the passageway. We won't leave you alone with her. You're the only person to bring her to justice. Be strong, Jessie, if not for you, do it for your kids."

The girls' faces fix in my mind. I take deep breaths, centering myself. I must do this. We need proof or I'll never see my kids again. I nod. "Okay, I'm ready. What do you want me to do?"

"I'll carry you into the room. Act sick or something. Like you're drugged maybe will be best. Yeah, I can work with that idea. Ready?" Alex swings me into his arms and shoulders his way into the room. "Help! I need help here. Somebody!"

FORTY-THREE

I push down panic as the familiar smells of my hospital room increase the closer I get to the bed. Each day, Maria wipes everything down with disinfectant as if I'm suffering from some incurable disease. The sharp pine scent burns my nostrils as Alex lowers me gently to the bed. I grip his shirt. "I need a drink of water."

"Okay." He scans the room and then gives me the water.

I drink, allowing the cool liquid to soothe my throat. I hand the bottle back and curl up on my side, facing the camera. Knowing it's there soothes my nerves a little but my heart is still pounding way too fast. I breathe slow and deep in an attempt to calm it. I need to center my mind on something nice and move my attention to the rose garden, and the sight is comfortingly familiar. The color of the blooms vary from deep blood red, to a buttery yellow, and from this angle I can see the new blue variety that Grandma included last year. Across the garden there are hundreds of flower heads spreading their petals in varying degrees to the sun and tight buds are evident all over, ensuring there are always blooms on display.

"Hey, is someone there?" Alex moves to the passageway and

stops with one hand resting on the doorframe. He raises his voice. "I need help in here. I have Jessie and she needs help."

Hurried footsteps come from the passageway and Dolly's voice pierces the quiet like a sergeant major's to the troops on a parade ground. I flinch but lie still. I must appear to be drugged or she will inject me with something horrible again.

"How did you get in here?" Dolly pushes her way into the room, dark eyes moving everywhere.

"Never mind. Jessie needs help." Alex's voice rises as he makes his point. "She's becoming more unstable by the minute and demanding to see her kids. I didn't know what to do. She just wouldn't listen to me so I called the paramedics and they gave her an injection to calm her down. They wanted to take her to the hospital and mentioned a psychiatric assessment. When I told them that she was under home care, with her own nurse, they wanted to transport her here but I insisted I'd bring her here right away." He sighs. "You'll be able to look after her, won't you?"

"Just how upset was she?" Dolly is standing so close to me I can smell the lemon hand lotion she uses.

"She was screaming and throwing things. She tried to steal my truck and she can hardly walk." Alex shrugs. "I'm not a doctor—she just went crazy—okay? Look, I'm not able to care for her anymore. She needs specialist around-the-clock care." He rubs his chin. "Why don't you call her asshole of a husband to look after her? I'm not responsible for her. I hardly know her."

"Maybe you shouldn't have kidnapped her in the first place?" Dolly attaches wires to my chest and puts a blood pressure cuff on my arm. "I can take it from here. See yourself out—and if you show up again, I'll call the cops."

I see Alex from under my lashes. He gives me a long look and then nods. As he walks away, fear of being alone with Dolly again grips me in waves of terror. The claustrophobic feeling of being trapped inside my body comes back in a rush. I fight to push down a tsunami of panic and the monitor goes crazy. Just having Dolly close by terrifies me. I know exactly what she can do. One apparent accidental overdose and all of Michael's dreams will come true. Right now, the will still stands. If I die, he gets everything.

FORTY-FOUR

I'm alone, helpless. If this doesn't work, I'll be dead and Michael has won.

"You've been a bad girl, haven't you?" Dolly rolls me onto my back. "Your brother will be here soon and we'll decide what to do with you. I know you tried to have him arrested. He's no fool. He knows his phone is being monitored, so he purchased a burner." She chuckles.

A tremble goes through me as I control the terror creeping up on me. Michael is coming here? I hope Alex overheard what she is saying. I breathe in and out slowly and try to relax. She pokes me, and not flinching is difficult. I'm afraid and so angry at her at the same time. She betrayed me and I fell for it hook, line, and sinker. I so wish I had my strength back but I'm weak; if she comes at me with a shot, I'm helpless to do anything.

"Everyone believes you've lost your mind. You've made it so easy for us. I can keep you here forever, living like a vegetable—well, long enough for Michael to have the estate transferred to him." She gets down close to my face and I can smell her onion breath. "If we come up with any complications and the estate doesn't go to him—you die."

She straightens, and I'm afraid she'll head back to her office. I take a chance and moan and thrash about. I'm risking another dose of the zombie drug but I must do this, John needs time to search her computer, although surely the video will catch her death threats—but what if it doesn't?

I get her attention and she checks the monitors again. I fall back into a stupor but she hovers over me, watching me. I feel like a mouse waiting for the cat to pounce and my heart rate spikes again. I moan again and toss my head around.

"What did they give you?" Dolly hits the button on the blood pressure machine and it tightens around my arm. "Your heart is racing. Maybe you're allergic to the medication. That's good, it will be a reason why you died. I can't be blamed, how sweet is that?"

I want to open my eyes and scream at her. This woman is supposed to care for people and what did it take to turn her into a monster—greed. I'm worth more dead than alive to Michael and no doubt he's offered her a life of luxury on my inheritance. How long has it been? Ten minutes maybe. Every second counts. I moan again and toss my head but under my lashes I see Dolly's attention move to the door leading to the conservatory. Has she seen Alex? My heart rate increases and I try to take deep calming breaths to prevent the machine screaming a warning.

Not Alex—Michael. My loving brother who wants me dead is heading straight toward me.

"She's back I see and where's John?" His voice is just above a whisper. "His Lexus is parked outside the conservatory. If he finds me here, all hell will break loose."

"I haven't seen him." Dolly turns to stare at the passageway. "It was the guy that kidnapped her. He brought her back. He said she went crazy and needed to be sedated."

"So why isn't John here to see Jessie? Surely Alex told him he'd brought her here?" Michael dashes a hand through his hair.

"There's only John's vehicle so Alex must have left." He turns to the passageway. "You sure you haven't seen or heard him?"

"Positive. No one is here apart from Maria." Dolly sighs. "She doesn't even know Mrs. Harper is here. She's probably in her room. You do know, she moved into the house from the cottage. She said it was on Mr. Harper's orders."

"We must finish this now before he shows. You know what to do." Michael grabs Dolly by the shoulders. "I need to get the heck out of here. Remove all the machines from her first. Do it and then head back to your room. You never saw Alex bring her back—right? The cops will blame everything on him. If John is here, he'll find her and then we'll be home free." He kisses her. "I know I can count on you, Dolly."

"Okay." Dolly turns away from him and removes the pads she stuck to my chest. "Go, it will be all over soon. She's very weak and her heart isn't good."

I hear footsteps as Michael, the brother I still love and once trusted, leaves me to die. A sob almost escapes and I smother it. How could he do this to me? I moan again and lift my hands up beside my head, hopefully making it harder for her to inject me with a fatal dose. I can't allow her to do it. I must find the strength to hold her off in time for Alex or John to save me.

I hear her go to the closet and can't see what she's doing from under my lashes. The drawer where she keeps the drugs is on the other side of the room and within view. What is she planning? She comes back carrying a pillow and panic rolls over me in waves. I must escape but as I open my mouth to scream, the pillow is over my face and I'm in terrible suffocating darkness.

All my childhood terrors grip me; fear of the dark, fear of monsters, fear of being buried alive rush at me in the darkness. I fight for a breath but fabric crushes my nose. My hands are beside my face and I push up as hard as I can. Dolly isn't expecting me to fight back and I get a second's reprieve as I push the pillow up an inch and suck in air. Blankets tangle around my legs as I kick and roll, trying to get free. The pillow is tight, the air is gone. My body is screaming for oxygen, my lungs hurt, bright spots flash in front of my eyes. My heart pounds and then misses beats. I'm drifting away. Oh God, I'll never get to hold my girls again—I'm so sorry, I can't fight anymore.

Light almost blinds me as the pillow is pulled free. My vision blurs as someone leans over me.

"Jessie." John's voice is in panic mode as he shakes me. I've never heard that before. "Jessie, breathe. Dear God, breathe."

I suck in a breath and then another and slowly everything comes back into focus. I want to speak and tell him everything is okay but I can't form words.

"That's right, big breaths." John sits me up. "Look at me, Jessie. You're safe."

John is holding me now and rubbing my back. Over his shoulder I see Alex gripping Dolly's arms behind her back; his eyes are wild and almost frantic. She has a bruise on one cheek. Did John or Alex hit her? I don't really care. The air is cooling down my burning throat. I take deep breaths but my head is fuzzy and my eyes are so sore. I don't want to lift my head from John's shoulder. The monsters are gone and suddenly everything is okay.

FORTY-FIVE

Paramedics check me over and the police take Dolly away. It takes forever but I insist I tell them my story although John is concerned. He wants a lawyer present, although I've done nothing wrong. I sit in the bed I hate, my prison, and answer countless questions. After a long time, I'm exhausted and lean back and close my eyes. "My head is spinning. I need a break."

"That's enough for tonight." John stands and moves between the detective and me. "Jessie is exhausted. She'll talk to you again, after she's had some rest. Maybe in a day or so."

The detective, whose name slipped from my memory the moment he uttered it, gives me an exasperated stare. I shrug and look away. I just want to be out of this place. As they leave, I look at John. I need his arms around me and hold them out to him. "Can you spare a hug?"

"You're so fragile, I'm frightened I might break you." He sits on the bed and puts one arm around me and then another. "Is that okay?" His phone buzzes and he sighs. "It's been going off all afternoon. It must be something important. Do you mind?"

I shake my head. "I guess not."

"It's wonderful news." John smiles at me. "The court rescinded the order. You can see the girls. It's over, Jessie."

I lean in and wrap my arms around him. I inhale the familiar scent of my husband and suddenly everything is right in the world—well, almost. "Can I please go home right away? I want to see the girls so bad."

"Yes. We'll leave right away. They'll be so happy to see you." John moves and turns to Alex. He offers him his hand. "Thank you so much for everything you've done for Jessie. You're a good friend, Alex."

"It's been an honor to know both of you." Alex shrugs. "I hope to see you back at the studio soon, Jessie."

"She'll be there and you're welcome at our home anytime." John smiles at him.

I look from one to the other in amazement. They really seem to get along. "I can't wait to get back to the studio. It's a lovely place to relax. As soon as I'm strong enough, I'll be there."

"Ready?" John scoops me up into his arms and carries me through the house. On the way, he stops to speak to Maria. "Take care of the house. You're in charge now and I'll increase your pay and add a bonus for everything you've done for my wife. Please get someone to collect all the medical equipment, we don't need it anymore. Call my office if you need anything, including staff."

"I will. Thank you, sir." Maria follows us to the front door.

The drive back to Grande Haven passes in a blur. All I can do is stare at John. I have him back. Although he has never left my heart. All my doubts and fears have vanished like the morning mist under a summer sun. I recognize the highway leading to my home, and as we pass through the Grande Haven gates, my heart races with anticipation. My girls will be asleep now but not for long; soon I'll get to see them, hug them, and smell their hair. I'm so excited my hands shake. John's Lexus slides into the garage and in seconds he's opening my door and carrying me inside. The familiar scents of my home surround me. My mom and dad come out of the family room to greet me. I can't stop the tears as familiar arms surround me in hugs. "I'm so happy to see you. Are my girls asleep?"

I hear a thundering on the stairs and turn to see the twins barreling down the steps with John on their heels. I turn, trembling with excitement, and hold out my arms. "Emily, Olivia."

"Momeeeee." Their smiles light up my heart.

They thump into me and I'm glad of my dad's strong arm for support. They hug me and I press kisses on their cheeks and stare at them in wonder. They're really here. My beautiful girls.

"We missed you so much." Olivia presses against my side, one hand fisted in my gown.

"Are you home for good now, Mommy?" Emily wipes tears from her rosy cheeks.

I hold them close, unable to let go for a second. "Yes, I'm home and everything is going to be just fine."

EPILOGUE

FOUR WEEKS LATER

It's hard to believe it's only four weeks since Dolly tried to kill me. I'm well, the broken blood vessels in my eyes have healed, and I look almost normal. My weight is good and the physical therapist has improved my fitness. Best of all I'm home with my girls. My parents are staying with us; I know it's an excuse to make sure I can cope alone. I'm almost a stranger to my kids who have grown like weeds but we're getting along just fine. I'm bursting with love for them. John and I are like newlyweds, and his new work schedule means we have more time together, although I did dump my portfolio on him.

I'm still good friends with Alex and will be starting back at art class again soon. He and John have become good friends and we and Alex's new girlfriend, Suzanna, spend much of our downtime together. It's like a new normality, a new life has emerged out of the tatters of a miserable existence that had all been engineered by my brother, but more of that later.

Of course, I was cleared of causing the accident. Michael's fingerprints were all over the steering wheel. The computer in Dolly's office confirmed there never was a doctor watching over me. The only emails were between her and Michael. The plan to get my inheritance had started way before the accident and was well recorded in the emails. When I didn't die in the wreck, and for the following year, I'd been asleep, Michael was in a panic. He needed to pay people and had almost run through his inheritance. Fearing being discovered and sent to jail, he encouraged John to switch off life support. They sent me to Grandma's house but when I still didn't die, Michael arranged for Dolly to take over. He needed to control my outcome and decided to wake me because he'd already laid down the ground-work to make me appear I was losing my mind and believed he could finish the job. It had almost worked.

After viewing the video and the evidence gathered by the auditors at the firm, Michael was charged with embezzlement and attempted murder along with Dolly. The justice system takes a long time to make their conclusions but since I changed my will again, I don't believe Michael or Dolly will be a problem for us anytime soon.

We've had many family meetings. The entire fiasco was a shock to my mom especially when my dad sat down with us and came clean about Andrea Long and her daughter Michelle. The story went this way: Michael met Andrea at a party and had no idea she was underage by a month or so. When Andrea discov-ered she was carrying his child, she contacted him but he stonewalled her, so she went to my father. At first, Dad believed she was a fortune hunter but after she divulged some personal information about Michael and threatened to go to the media, Dad agreed to support her until the baby was born. After a DNA test proved her case, he went to Michael who swore he didn't remember meeting her. The chance of being charged would ruin his career, so Dad decided to continue to support Andrea and her child. He set up a trust fund for Michelle. However, since her birth, Dad has become attached to her and wants Michelle included in our family. We all agreed.

Everything came to a head the night Grandma died. She'd

decided to confront my dad after receiving the report from the private detective. It all started when my grandma's friend ran into Dad in a restaurant when he was dining with Andrea. Dad suspects she went straight to Grandma to spread the gossip and Grandma took it from there. She flung the accusations and the photographs from the private detective into my dad's face and fired him. Hearing what had happened, Michael used Grandma for his own ends to make her change her will. He turned her against John with the same lies he fed me. She went to her grave believing John and my dad were unfaithful.

I have no desire to live at Stonebridge Manor—not for some time, at least. The strange things that happened there still haunt me, hovering in the back of my mind like the bad dreams you can never forget. Maybe one day we'll all gather there for the holidays again to trim the tree and make new happy memories. In the meantime, it will be kept pristine by a proficient staff. There is one thing that remains a mystery: the phones throughout Grandma's house were never disconnected—I guess, I must be a little crazy after all.

A LETTER FROM D.K. HOOD

Dear Readers,

Thanks so much for choosing my novel and coming with me in *The Liar I Married*, my very first psychological thriller. I've enjoyed writing Jessie Harper's harrowing story. Being inside her head and unravelling her trauma was an exciting experience.

If you'd like to keep up to date with all my latest releases, just sign up at the website link below. Your details will never be shared and you can unsubscribe at any time.

www.bookouture.com/dk-hood

If you enjoyed my story, I would be very grateful if you could leave a review and recommend my book to your friends and family. I really enjoy hearing from readers so feel free to ask me questions at any time. You can get in touch on my Facebook page, my Facebook Reader's Group, or my webpage.

You'll be able to download a free copy of my short thriller, *In the Dead of Night*, a Detectives Kane and Alton story.

Thank you so much for your support.

D.K. Hood

KEEP IN TOUCH WITH D.K. HOOD

www.dkhood.com

 facebook.com/dkhoodauthor
x.com/DKHood_Author

ACKNOWLEDGMENTS

Many thanks to my editor, Helen, and #TeamBookouture. Your support and encouragement as I take my first steps into a new genre is inspiring.

PUBLISHING TEAM

Turning a manuscript into a book requires the efforts of many people. The publishing team at Bookouture would like to acknowledge everyone who contributed to this publication.

Audio
Alba Proko
Sinead O'Connor
Melissa Tran

Commercial
Lauren Morrissette
Hannah Richmond
Imogen Allport

Cover design
Emma Graves

Data and analysis
Mark Alder
Mohamed Bussuri

Editorial
Helen Jenner
Ria Clare